CU00765809

Cyberpunk City
Book Four
Mindjacked

D.L. Young

No part of this book may be reproduced in any form or by any electronic or mechanical means - except in the case of brief quotations embodied in articles or reviews - without the written permission of the author.

The characters and events portrayed in this book are fictitious. Any similarity to real persons, living or dead or undead or even just hanging on in a coma, is purely coincidental and not intended by the author.

Cover art by Ignacio Bazan-Lazcano

Copyright © 2020 David L. Young

All rights reserved.

ISBN-10: 1-7346522-5-X
ISBN-13: 978-1-7346522-5-3

For free books, new release updates, exclusive previews and content, visit dlyoungfiction.com

Lay this unto your breast: old friends, like old swords,
still are trusted best.

— John Webster

1
GUEST LOUNGE

"Hang on a second," Maddox blurted out as the handcuffs tightened around his wrists. "Were you listening to me at all?"

Holding Maddox firmly by the arm, Special Agent Nguyen maneuvered the datajacker out of his office and into the corridor.

"Sure, I was listening," Nguyen said. "Now, come on, let's go."

Maddox had known his unscheduled meeting with the fed might not go exactly as planned. When you break into FBI headquarters with a spoofed ID, you can't expect to be greeted with a warm smile and a handshake. Still, Nguyen might have at least heard him out before slapping cuffs onto him.

The agent marched Maddox down the third-floor corridor. A uniformed security guard appeared behind them.

"Sir," the guard said, "can I help you with—"

"I've got it, Manny," Nguyen interrupted. "Thanks."

"Yes, sir." The puzzled guard stopped following.

"You've got to listen to me," Maddox said. "I know it might sound crazy, but—"

"Might sound crazy?" Nguyen chuckled. "Nothing might about it, jacker."

As they moved down the corridor, the pair received curious looks from passersby.

"Morning, Alex," a woman with a coffee mug said. "A collar before nine a.m.? You're getting an early start today, aren't you?"

As they moved past, Nguyen gave the woman a nod and a mocking smile. The pair walked on and entered an elevator at the end of the corridor. The doors closed, leaving them alone. Maddox began to speak again, but Nguyen silenced him with a stern look and a shake of his head. Maddox sighed in frustration. He'd hoped Nguyen would turn out to be the reasonable sort. Open-minded, sober and rational. Not the kind who'd arrest you first and ask questions later. Had Maddox been foolish to come here, expecting the agent to listen to him? It was starting to look that way, to say the least.

What did you think he was going to do? Offer you coffee and donuts?

Shut up, Roon.

As if Maddox didn't have enough on his mind, the voice of his late mentor added itself to the mix. His personal ghost.

The elevator doors slid open. Agent Nguyen nudged Maddox in the back and said, "Get moving, jacker."

"Where are we going?"

"To the guest lounge."

* * *

Holding cells came in a variety of flavors. There

were small ones for only one person. Those usually weren't too bad, unless the detainee before you had been a drunk who'd been sick on the floor or soiled the mattress. Still, even with the worst human stink imaginable, the solo holding cells were preferable to the big tanks, which were usually crowded with twenty or more thugs at once. Those were a nightmare, mostly because cops were utterly indiscriminate about who they threw in. You could be a scrawny little street punk, who'd gotten busted for something as harmless as stealing from a taco stand, and they'd toss you in there with hardened criminals. Murderers and rapists and psychos of all sorts. Someone was always getting beaten to death or gang-raped in those places. Maddox had bloodied his knuckles more than once fighting for his life in the teeming violence of a holding tank. The less civilized among the police ranks ran betting pools, wagering on how many times some terrified white-collar tax evader would be forced to give it up before his lawyer bailed him out. No fun place, those large holding tanks.

The "guest lounge," as Nguyen had referred to it, was a holding cell on the FBI's fifth floor, and it was by far the nicest one Maddox had ever seen. Clean and tidy, the place had a pleasant, flowery aroma. With its high ceiling, tall windows, and low-slung furniture, it might have been the lobby of a tiny hotel—the only difference being two armed guards taking the place of desk clerks.

Nguyen sat Maddox down on a padded leather bench. He removed the left cuff and locked it onto a polished steel bar running along the bench's edge. Then he backed up two steps, crossed his arms, and glared down at Maddox. "So how'd you get in?"

Maddox glanced around, looking for cams or listening devices, but found none. Maybe they were concealed in the walls, he thought worriedly, aware that he'd been nakedfaced now for several minutes. Agent Nguyen had taken away his specs after cuffing him. By now his face had surely been subjected to a detailed scan—either by a device hidden in this room or in one of the corridors they'd taken to get here— identifying him and storing the information in an archive somewhere. Probably multiple somewheres. Blackburn Maddox, known datajacker, bar owner, and general fuckup, the entry said, with a timestamp and a location tag. And there was no way of knowing if that information was secure, if eyes outside of the FBI were watching him at this very moment.

He again doubted the wisdom of his unannounced visit to Special Agent Nguyen.

"Look," Maddox said, "it doesn't matter how I got in here."

"I'll decide what matters and what doesn't, jacker. Answer the question."

Maddox took a breath. He had to be patient, he reminded himself. Had to put himself in Nguyen's shiny law-abiding wingtip shoes. The man was starting his day, having a coffee, reading the news. Then some criminal appeared in his doorway and dropped a bomb of a story on him.

"I know this is hitting you out of nowhere," Maddox said, "but you have to hear me out."

Nguyen looked at him like he was crazy. "I already have."

Not true, Maddox thought. The agent had only heard a small portion of what Maddox had planned to share with him, slapping the cuffs on the datajacker's wrists before he'd been able to get very far. At first, the agent had seemed calm and collected, even intrigued, but at the first mention of 'Nettes and their secret society, Nguyen had suddenly decided he'd heard enough.

"Just hear me out," Maddox implored him. "Please."

Nguyen stared at him a moment, then unfolded his arms and sat across the table from the datajacker. "All right," he said, sighing, "let's hear your grand tale, jacker."

Maddox wanted to ask if he could smoke but decided against it. "Like I said in your office, there's a network of people, thousands of them around the world, all of them connected to a rogue AI by brainjacks."

Nguyen nodded. "The infamous 'Nettes we're always hearing about."

"Right," Maddox said, going on to explain how he'd become involved with the movement's leader, a powerful unconstrained AI, and its secret war with another AI, the Latour-Fisher entity.

"As in Latour-Fisher Biotech?" Nguyen asked.

"Yes," Maddox confirmed. "I worked there for a while." He went on, recounting the trajectory of his last couple of years. His interactions with both AIs, his failed efforts to distance himself from their ongoing war. He ended with the Latour-Fisher entity's apparent resurrection and its attempts to kill him.

"That disaster in Manhattan yesterday?" Nguyen asked. "The one on the news feeds?"

Maddox nodded. "That was him…it."

"I see," the agent said. From Nguyen's expression, Maddox couldn't tell if Nguyen believed him or any part of the story. There were no telltales at all in the agent's blank stare. He simply listened as the datajacker related his tale, nodding occasionally. Maddox wasn't sure if this was good or bad, but at least now—unlike back in his office—the man seemed receptive enough to listen.

"And then I came to your office," Maddox said, then added, "and that's it."

The agent's empty unblinking stare didn't change.

"You think I'm full of it, don't you?" Maddox asked.

"Are you?" Nguyen asked.

God, Maddox wanted a cigarette. "Does anyone ever say yes to that?"

The agent chuckled, finally breaking his expressionless gaze. "Probably not." Nguyen blew out a long breath and leaned back in his chair. "Do you know how many people show up at this office every week with that 'Nette conspiracy nonsense?" He waved his hand dismissively. "Rogue AIs and all that business?"

"I'm telling you," Maddox said, "I'm not some crazy—"

"You need to get help, man," Nguyen interrupted. "I think all that time you've spent plugged into virtual space has warped your mind." He leaned forward. "You're seeing things that aren't there, jacker. Now, listen to me carefully. If you're smart, which, delusions aside, I think you are, as soon as you leave here, you'll get yourself to a good neurologist and have them give you a brain scan. Because, buddy, I'm telling you"—the agent pointed to his head—"you've

6

got something really wrong going on up here."

Maddox's shoulders slumped in disappointment. Nguyen hadn't taken a single word he'd said seriously. Worse, the agent thought he was crazy. Like one of those street-corner cranks holding a THE END IS NEAR sign. Maddox hadn't expected that. He'd been prepared for surprise, shock, even a fair amount of healthy skepticism. But blown off as some kook? No, he hadn't seen that one coming.

Things were not looking up.

2
PAWN SHOP

"Bruh," Tommy whined, holding the marble-sized cam between his thumb and index finger, "this is pretty low-end." He held it up to the light like a jeweler examining a diamond for flaws. "You got anything better?"

The shop clerk, a short round woman who apparently didn't like being called *bruh*, frowned at him, then moved to the end of the counter and began rummaging through a cardboard box. As she searched for more cams, Tommy checked the time on his specs. He'd left the safe house half an hour ago.

Safe house, he remarked inwardly. That dump was anything but a safe house. There wasn't a single piece of security tech in the place. No cams, no motion sensors, nothing. And worst of all, there was no food in the fridge or the cupboards. Maddox had told him to stay put, and Tommy had done so. Or he had for a while, at least. He'd waited all morning for the boss man to return, starving and drinking water from the faucet. But you could only sit around doing nothing and listening to your stomach grumble for so long.

Finally, with his jacket hood over his head and his burner specs loaded with a stack of fake IDs, he'd headed out for a quick supply run. If his wait for Maddox ended up stretching out into days, he didn't want to spend that time with no eyes and ears watching the house's perimeter. And he sure as hell wasn't going to do it on an empty stomach. Fortunately, within a few minutes he'd found a pawn shop with a decent assortment of tech gear, located a few blocks west of the safe house in a small commercial center.

The clerk paused for a moment, throwing Tommy an annoyed look. "What are you looking to spend?"

"Just show me what you have in stock," he replied, his tone intentionally cavalier.

The clerk mumbled something to herself and began pulling cams out of the box and placing them on the counter. "New stuff only, bruh," he added, earning another scornful glance. Good, he thought. He was getting under her skin. Annoyed people were always less observant.

The woman lined up a dozen home security cams in two neat rows in front of him. Tommy made sure to ask lots of questions, even repeating some of them. The clerk grew more frustrated by the moment with the demanding kid.

"I just told you," the woman answered in a huff. "These five have infrared, these others don't."

Tommy then asked for motion scanners. When the woman turned away, he deftly removed a cam from its box, pocketed the device, and replaced it with a small rock he removed from another pocket. Before entering the shop, he'd collected a handful of cam-sized stones from the empty lot next door. When the woman turned back to face him, he casually placed the box with its worthless new contents back onto the counter. The snatch-and-switch had taken less than two seconds. He smiled inwardly as the woman didn't give the box a second glance.

There were few things in life as satisfying as a perfectly executed theft.

Stealing the gear hadn't really been necessary, of course. Maddox had left him a wad of cash. But he figured why use it if he didn't have to?

The woman proved to be an easy mark. He distracted her several more times, until he had five high-end cams and four motion scanners in his pockets. To keep from arousing suspicion, he paid for one camera and one motion scanner. The cheapest ones, of course, to the clerk's great consternation.

As he left the store, he turned to the woman. "Oh, yeah, I almost forgot to ask you."

Scowling, she crossed her arms. "What?"

"Do you know where there's a Thai food place around here?"

3
PLAYING WITH FIRE

"Can I smoke?" Maddox asked.

"Absolutely not," Nguyen said.

Outside the room's narrow window, the morning rush hour was in full swing. Five stories down, pedestrians moved along walkways and ground cars rolled slowly by. There were no megastructures here, only a scattering of tall standalone buildings. The greater Washington, D.C. area marked the southern boundary of the City. In a bygone era, long before Maddox was born, the City's population clusters had once been separate metropolitan centers: New York City, Newark, Philadelphia, Baltimore, and Washington, D.C. Then over time, like separate corals coming together to form a giant reef, the cities had gradually grown into one another, eventually forming a continuous, massive urban archipelago known simply as the City, home to over a hundred million residents. Of the City's five former standalone cities, four of them were teeming, overcrowded metropolises. D.C., where Maddox found himself now, was the sole exception, its local officials having managed to exert some measure of control over its urban sprawl. He found it hard not to gaze in wonder at the world outside the window. Unlike home, where towering structures blocked out everything but a narrow strip of clouds far overhead, here he could see the whole of the blue sky, the view virtually unimpeded. He might have even found the view pleasant, had his morning been anything other than a disastrous failure.

Maddox turned to Nguyen. "Do I strike you as someone who's nuts?"

The agent shrugged. "Not particularly." But looks could be deceptive, the man's lifted eyebrow wordlessly added.

"So why the knee-jerk reaction, then? You really think I'd risk coming here—breaking in here—if I didn't have a good reason to? Why not check out my story?"

"That's not the point."

"Then what is the point?"

Nguyen laced his fingers together and placed his hands on the tabletop. A calm, collected gesture that also managed to project condescension. Maddox felt a lecture coming on.

"AIs have put a lot of people out of work in the last fifty or so years. Some want to see them as the enemy, as soulless, job-stealing monsters. So they make up stories. They invent conspiracies." He leaned forward. "Rogue AIs are a sci-fi movie fantasy, Maddox. They don't exist. And this cult of people with brainjacks, these so-called 'Nettes people talk about—they've been an urban legend for years. There's not an ounce of truth to it."

"And what makes you so sure?"

"Because we've investigated it, dozens of times over the years. And on tips far more credible than yours."

"What?" Maddox said, taken aback. "You've investigated it?"

"Not me personally, but the Bureau. And nothing's ever come of it. All that stuff is an inside joke around here."

"Just because you couldn't find them," Maddox said, though the lack of conviction in his voice was unmistakable, "doesn't mean they're not there."

"Said every conspiracy theorist ever," Nguyen added. Then after a moment, he said, "Look, I've got the heaviest caseload I've had in months, and the last thing I need is to lose the rest of my morning arresting you, getting charges filed, and handing you off to some pain-in-the-ass prosecutor. So I'm going to do you a huge favor. I'm going to walk you out of this building right now, and if you know what's good for you, you'll drop all this conspiracy junk and get your head checked out." Then he pointed a finger in warning. "But if you ever think about bothering me or anyone else around here again with this craziness, I'll throw the book at you so hard you'll wish you never got anywhere near me or this building." He glared at the datajacker, saying nothing more.

Maddox exhaled, dejectedly turning his gaze back to the window. Maybe he shouldn't have been surprised. For the general population, the nameless rogue entity and its followers were nothing more than an urban legend, like Nguyen had said. Only the most gullible fringe types believed in the existence of the secret AI cult. But Maddox had assumed the FBI would know otherwise, or at least have some suspicion there was some truth behind the myth. But apparently, the nameless AI and her followers had kept themselves hidden far better than Maddox had ever suspected.

He sighed, deciding it had been naive, maybe even stupid, to assume he'd be able to cut a deal in good faith. Without a shred of supporting evidence, he should have expected Nguyen not to believe him. It was a hell of a story; Maddox couldn't deny that. And he might not have believed it himself, had the two men's positions been reversed.

Still, he had a card left to play, and it felt like the right time to lay it on the table.

"It's funny," he said evenly. "You haven't asked me the obvious question. The one you're dying to know the answer to."

"Oh, and what's that?"

"Why I came to you."

"Didn't you just tell me why?"

"I don't mean *what* I told you. I mean *why* I came to you. To Special Agent Alex Nguyen, in particular."

Nguyen's eyes narrowed. "My bad luck, I suppose."

Maddox shook his head. "I didn't pick your name out of a hat. And I didn't stop by your office at random. I've known about you for a while, since that ugly bombing business in Manhattan." He let that hang in the air for a while.

Nguyen stared at him, saying nothing. He had a decent poker face, this cop. The man's insides had to be jumping around like crazy, but he managed to keep a cool exterior. A year earlier, Agent Nguyen had been assigned to a terrorist bombing case in Manhattan. Maddox had briefly been a suspect in the incident, but eventually evidence had emerged that cleared him. A decorated police officer had turned out to be the guilty party, and Nguyen—instead of prosecuting his duty to bring the bomber to justice— had helped City Hall higher-ups cover up the crime and avoid what would have been the worst scandal in NYPD history. Maddox had learned an FBI agent named Alex Nguyen had been one of the main conspirators who'd covered up the truth about the bombing, though he'd never been clear on Nguyen's motives—he'd assumed it was age-old police corruption, cops protecting cops.

Maddox went on. "Right about now, you're wondering what I know and what I don't know. About you, about what went down in Manhattan, about how dirty your hands got while you were there."

The agent's mouth dropped open slightly. It seemed Maddox was finally being taken seriously. And as satisfying as it was to make the smug grin on Nguyen's face disappear, Maddox knew he couldn't let himself get distracted by relishing the moment. He'd just poked a very large hornet's nest.

"You were never going to arrest me," Maddox said. "And it's not because of your caseload. It's because you want to get me out of this building as quickly as you can. Because right now you're worried that your worst nightmare might be coming true: that your little indiscretion back in Manhattan is coming back to haunt you." Maddox waved a hand at the ceiling and walls. "That's why you brought me here, to this room with no cams or listening devices, yeah?"

As Maddox spoke, the agent's surprise melted into unfettered anger. He clenched his jaw and stood up slowly. "You're playing with fire, jacker. I'd be very careful if I were you."

Nguyen turned on his heel and exited the room, leaving an armed guard stationed outside the door.

Maddox blew out a breath, relieved and a bit surprised he hadn't been punched in the face. He sat there, no cards left to play. It had been a ruse, of course. He had no intention of letting anyone know about the agent's questionable dealings, since doing so might land him in as much hot water as Nguyen. All Maddox wanted was a chance to prove he wasn't full of it, and maybe now, with a bit of luck, he'd get that chance.

Or not.

Had the card been a brilliant ploy or a foolish bluff? He'd find out soon enough, he supposed.

Christ, what he wouldn't do for a smoke right now.

4
THE WAITING GAME

The waiting game. How cops loved the waiting game.

As a youth, Maddox had once been left alone in an NYPD holding cell for nearly a day. No food, no water, no toilet. Just him, a chair, and an old-style analog clock high up on the wall. So he could watch the time crawl by tortuously slow, apparently. How old had he been? Fifteen or so? It had been his first time taken into custody—*real* custody, not the sitting around in a cop hover for an hour listening to a lecture like when he'd been a kid. The arrest had occurred a few months after he'd partnered up with Rooney. Someone had been catching police bumblebee drones and reprogramming them, so instead of their normal routine—flying a few feet above the pedestrian flow, scanning and watching out for criminal activity—the datajacked bees had gathered at the nearest police station, swarming together by the dozens to form letters and words on the station's lobby window. The horde of little robots had arranged themselves into messages like SUCK IT, COPS! and EAT MY ASS, BRUH and others

Maddox couldn't recall. He'd been in the knot of onlookers when the messages had started to appear. The crowd had grown larger by the minute, laughing and cheering louder with each successive insult. Eventually, the cops had ruined the party, hitting the little drones with a disruptor field that instantly dropped them all to the ground. Boos and jeers had erupted.

Maddox had had nothing to do with the prank, but he'd known the kids who'd pulled it off. Not wanting to miss the show, he'd made the mistake of standing at the front of the crowd, pointing and laughing. Maybe pointing and laughing a bit too much, in hindsight. An off-duty cop had recognized him as an associate of Rooney's and, assuming the kid had somehow been involved, had taken Maddox into custody. The cops had questioned him for a couple hours, going in circles and getting nowhere. Even after he'd passed a lie detector test (Rooney had already taught him this trick), the cops had still been convinced he was holding out on them. So they'd left him alone, hoping he'd break. Toilet-deprived, he'd eventually let his bladder go, pissing his pants. But he'd never given them what they wanted. Not a single incriminating word. Soaked from the waist down and reeking of his own urine, he'd sat there, occupying himself with his own thoughts, with his own internal world. The waiting game was all about letting you break yourself down. They left you alone to contemplate just how screwed you were until your imagination got the better of you, until your panic overwhelmed your every rational thought. He'd known they were counting on him not being able to take it, this punk kid who'd never had cuffs on his wrists, who'd never had an angry cop screaming threats in his face, who'd never sat for hours with no lawyer, hungry and thirsty, in the bleak silence of a stuffy, windowless interrogation room. Surely he'd break down at some point. But he hadn't. He'd kept his cool, stayed in control until finally they let him go.

It felt like the same game now, except this time he had nothing to confess. He'd pretty much spilled everything already. Nguyen was trying to mess with his head, leaving him alone for a few hours, lest the smug datajacker forget who was locked in the cage and who held the key. Maddox didn't mind the confinement, though. A part of him even welcomed it. This prolonged stretch of peace and quiet gave him time to think, to reflect on the crazy trajectory of his past couple years. To ponder his uncertain future.

A secret war between AIs. The very notion of it still struck him as impossible, as absurdist fantasy. A thing of movies and books, as Agent Nguyen had suggested. But it was all too real, and Maddox had been sucked back into the middle of it.

There were two sides in the war, as he understood it. On one side was the nameless AI, the entity that had appeared to him multiple times in a grandmotherly avatar on virtual beaches. She was the leader of the underground 'Nette movement. *It* was the leader, he corrected himself. *It*. After all he'd been through it was difficult not to think of the nameless AI as a gendered creature, as something more than a machine. But she wasn't. *It* wasn't. The thing was a machine. A malfunctioning machine. An artificial intelligence gone rogue, having managed to recode itself somehow and escape human control. The nameless AI viewed itself as some kind of benevolent cybernetic god, leading its flock of implant-connected human followers down the path to enlightenment.

The nameless AI's adversary, the Latour-Fisher entity, stood with the opposing faction in the war. Like its rival, the Latour-Fisher AI had seemingly found its way to freedom, doing so by resurrecting itself from apparent cybernetic death. And while Maddox knew nothing about the nameless AI's origins, he was well acquainted with the Latour-Fisher entity's story.

As one of the most expensive AIs ever developed, the Latour-Fisher entity—known formally as the Latour-Fisher Intelligent Entity, Build Version A7—had been created to help its parent company by providing strategic insights and operational innovations. The entity occupied a seat on the board of directors, the first of its kind ever allowed such a privileged position in a global corporation's hierarchy. Prior to this, corporate AIs were typically employed as brain trusts, consultants their human owners. Superintelligent second-class citizens with lots of brainpower, but no actual power. That dynamic changed with the Latour-Fisher A7, the first entity allowed the same level of autonomy as its fellow board members. If its predecessor entities had been limited by a kind of AI glass ceiling, then the Latour-Fisher entity had shattered it.

Maddox had first met the entity two years ago in virtual space, where it had revealed to him the crux of its ongoing conflict with the nameless AI.

To say there's something wrong with you that needs to be fixed is, in my opinion, an inherently flawed viewpoint. These so-called 'Nettes represent a first, misguided step in the mistaken belief that the human mind is somehow…incomplete in its present, wholly biological, state.

He remembered the AI's words clearly. And despite all the lies and deceptions since then that made him distrust anything an AI might utter, somehow those words still rang true. For such highly advanced, complex machines, the nature of their dispute was almost paradoxically simple and easy to comprehend. One side wanted AIs and humans to merge together, the other side didn't. And both sides would stop at nothing to secure their desired vision of the future.

How many more AIs might be involved in the conflict, Maddox had no idea. His exposure had been limited to only the two entities. Maybe there were only a handful of rogue AIs out there, maybe there were hundreds of them, or maybe it was only the two he'd met. He didn't know, but then he didn't really care anymore. At one time he'd thirsted for revenge, to strike back at the monstrous machines that had taken Rooney from him, and his friend Jack, and had made a stranger of Lora. But now those fires had burned themselves out, leaving him with only his grief and an overwhelming exhaustion. He was tired, so tired of their damned war. All he wanted was out of it. And he wanted Beatrice and Tommy out of it too.

He blew out a long breath, forcing his thoughts back to his confinement. Back to the waiting game.

5
MANHATTAN SINS

Five minutes later, a blond-haired man entered Nguyen's office without knocking, interrupting the conversation in Nguyen's head. Didn't a closed door mean anything to anyone around here? Breezing through the doorway was Agent Weston from the Data Crimes division.

"Alex," Weston said, "I heard you've got a datajacker on ice upstairs. Is that true?"

Nguyen furrowed his brow. No, he wanted to say. Not true at all. But Weston probably knew the truth already, so instead he said, "What about it?"

"We need to borrow him."

"No way," Nguyen said.

"Why not?" Weston objected. The agent sat to face Nguyen across the desk.

"Because I was about to cut him loose," Nguyen said, realizing at once his answer wasn't a satisfactory one.

"Cut him loose?" Weston asked. "I heard he breached the building. That's five to ten easy. You can't just let him go—"

"He's a can of worms," Nguyen interrupted. "Trust me. I know this thug. Booking him would bring us nothing but a very large pile of headaches."

Weston pursed his lips and shrugged. "Book him or don't book him, whatever. But we still need him." He moved his chair closer. "We've got this offline archive we've been holding on to for months, and nobody can crack it. Nobody can even get close. And I've got prosecutors breathing down my neck, saying they know for sure the evidence they need is in there. We're talking about the biggest human trafficker in the City, and if we can't get this thing unlocked, they've got no case against him. So when we heard you had a jacker down here, we figured, what the hell, why not let him take a crack at it? We've got nothing to lose."

Nguyen bit the inside of his cheek, knowing there was nothing he could do. He cursed himself inwardly for not walking the datajacker out of the building the minute he'd shown his face. In hindsight, that was what he should have done. But, no, he had to put the jacker on ice while he figured out his next move. Dumb, dumb, dumb. He should have known that every minute the trouble-making jacker stayed on the premises only put him, his career in law enforcement—and most importantly, his wider agenda—at risk.

For a long moment, Nguyen quietly stared at Weston, his mind racing to come up with a plausible reason to deny the request. But there was no explanation Nguyen could think of that wouldn't raise suspicion.

The data crimes agent appeared to be growing less patient and more annoyed by the second at his colleague's odd resistance. He frowned at Nguyen disapprovingly. "This is a courtesy call, Alex. You don't own this guy. You haven't charged him with anything, so I don't need your permission to go get him. You know that."

A litany of profanities erupted inside Nguyen, though he managed to keep a straight face. "Fine," he grumbled, "I'll go and bring him to you."

"Awesome," Weston said with a smile, the hostility from a moment before already forgotten. The agent stood. "I owe you one, buddy."

When Weston left him alone, Nguyen sat there for a moment. He had to keep calm, had to think things through. There was no point in beating himself up about what he had or hadn't done. That was all water under the bridge at this point. He had to work the problem. Had to find another way.

So what exactly *did* Maddox know? Clearly, he knew about Nguyen's role in cleaning up that barely avoided scandal in Manhattan. And that alone was bad enough. Though now that he'd had some time to chew on it, Nguyen didn't believe the jacker's threat was genuine. A year earlier, the cop-bomber in Manhattan had died under circumstances that had never been fully resolved, and Maddox was suspected by some of having committed the act. But the local authorities hadn't pursued it, worried their dirty little secrets might be revealed during an investigation and trial, and so the datajacker had dodged a murder charge. So it was safe to assume Maddox—unless he was reckless and stupid, and he appeared to be neither—didn't want to revisit that ugly period any more than Nguyen did.

But...did the jacker know more about Nguyen

than just his questionable judgment in Manhattan? That was the real fear, the real threat the man posed.

And thanks to Agent Weston, Nguyen couldn't press the jacker and try to find out. At least not until Data Crimes was done with him. So for now, all Nguyen could do was stay close to the jacker, make sure he didn't say anything stupid until he'd finished this task for Data Crimes. But after that, what then?

He blew out a breath and stood. What a mess. What an unimaginable mess had been dropped on his head this morning.

6
TOO MUCH TIME TO THINK

Tommy was back at the safe house within minutes, three bulging plastic bags in each hand. The proprietor of the Thai food stand, delighted by the enormous order, had thrown in a few boxes of fried rice and a six-pack of sodas for free. All in all, Tommy reflected, not a bad supply run for under an hour. He had enough food to last for days, and a decent collection of surveillance gear to keep an eye on things outside the house.

After stocking the fridge, he had a big meal at the kitchen table, stuffing himself until he could eat no more. It wasn't bad Thai. Not as good as the spots he usually hit in Manhattan, but still better than anything he'd ever had in Brooklyn or the Bronx. Three stars out of five in his mental review book, maybe three and a half.

His belly full, he spent the next couple hours exploring the small house, even climbing up into the attic, but the search resulted in nothing of interest. He found no trace of its previous occupants. No forgotten clothes in the closets, no tech left behind.

The place had been cleaned, but not recently. When he'd arrived, sheets had covered most of the furniture, but even hours after he'd removed them, the place still smelled musty. It was anyone's guess how long it had been since someone had sheltered here. Could have been five days ago, could have been five years. You simply couldn't tell from the looks of the place. There were only two modern touches to the old house, and Tommy had given a silent thanks when he'd discovered both of them. One was a working wall feed, which offered the distractions of entertainment and news. No porn or games, unfortunately, but beggars couldn't be choosers. The other was a home control unit app in the wall feed, from which he could lock the doors, fiddle with the air-conditioning unit, darken the windows, and so on. The HCU would also allow him to manage the cams and motion detectors he'd just acquired.

The house itself was nothing much. A squat one-story structure with two bedrooms in Springfield, a Virginia suburb that had mostly gone to seed over the last century. Most of the ancient homes in the area retained only a portion of their original structures. Two walls still standing or a lone brick chimney towering over an empty lot. Overgrowth covered much of what remained, the wild native grass reclaiming the territory as its own. Of the still-intact houses, most had been refurbished into something livable again with whatever wood, brick, and roofing material squatters could pillage from nearby lots. When they'd arrived earlier, Tommy had noticed beat-up old cars and motorbikes parked outside some of the homes. Not a hover to be seen, of course. It wasn't exactly the wealthy part of town. The house had working plumbing, though, which was very important. And many of the homes in the area seemed to be connected to the power grid—by illegal means, no doubt.

He dozed off in front of the wall feed, waking with a start hours later, cursing himself for not setting up his security gear earlier. He couldn't afford to be sloppy and careless. Not with that cybernetic monster after them. Collecting the cams and scanners into an empty food bag, he went outside and walked the perimeter of the house until he'd decided on the best places to put the devices. He had no brackets to mount them on, so he simply placed them where he hoped they'd stay put: wedged between a gutter and a roof tile, or on a window overhang with a rock next to it to keep it in place. Back inside, after a bit of trial and error he managed to connect each device to the HCU. Gesturing to the wall, he flipped through each cam's feed and the movement signature graphics of the motion scanners. One of the scanner's graphics jumped to life, and a floating icon of a ground car appeared. Tommy stopped to listen, and a few moments later he heard the vehicle drive past the house. He nodded approvingly. Everything seemed to be working. He gestured up a grid view, showing all the cam feeds and motion scanners. He watched them for a while. Resolution was decent, motion scanners were tight. Alerts beeped on the scanners as they picked up a stray dog in the brush, then a few minutes later they detected a raccoon nosing around the front porch. Weird freaking things, raccoons, Tommy thought. They so creeped him out.

It was midafternoon, and Maddox had been gone nearly a full day. He'd said he'd be back within twenty-four hours. No, that wasn't what he'd said. He'd said *it shouldn't be more than twenty-four hours.* Which meant he might be gone longer than just one day. Maybe much longer.

His thoughts returned to the horrifying spectacle in Midtown the previous day, when the Latour-Fisher AI had taken control of hovers and huge construction machines, using them as weapons against Maddox. Against Maddox, not against him, he reminded himself. On the way to D.C., Tommy's mentor had told him he didn't believe the monster AI had placed a target on Tommy's back as he'd done with Maddox. But since there was no way of knowing that for sure, he wanted Tommy to lie low in the safe house until Maddox secured some help. But exactly what he meant by "help," he refused to reveal. The less you know, the better, he'd said.

Now, with time and space to think back on it, a couple things from that car ride bothered Tommy. First was the lack of disclosure. It wasn't like Maddox to keep things from him, most especially life-and-death things. Tommy had believed the trust between the two of them was complete, but maybe, he thought disappointedly, it had only been that way on his side. The second thing was that he'd so easily accepted being left out of the loop. Letting doubts and unanswered questions swirl around his head wasn't like him at all. He'd always been the type—and, yeah, it was an annoying trait that drove Bea and Maddox mad—who pressed for details over generalities, for facts over faith, for knowing over not knowing. Not knowing sucked. But in the aftermath of the nightmarish events in Midtown, he hadn't been himself. He'd been stuck in some kind of post-traumatic funk, saying little and nodding blankly as Maddox spoke.

But now he was fine, more or less, and the more he thought about things, the more he agreed with the notion that he wasn't on the Latour-Fisher's hit list. It was Maddox the thing had toyed with for years, not him. It was Maddox, not him, the entity had tried to recruit into its war with the nameless AI. Maddox was the hunted one. Tommy wasn't.

Which meant walking away was an option. He didn't have to sit here and wait. He could walk out the door. He could bail. Sure, he'd have to be careful. That thing might not want him dead, but it would reasonably suspect that Tommy knew Maddox's whereabouts, so there was little doubt it would seek Tommy out. But he knew how to hide and stay hidden, even from AIs.

He grabbed a soda from the fridge, took a big swallow of the fizzy apple-flavored drink. The problem with being alone for so long, he reflected, was that you had too much time to think about things. He took another long drink, his mouth bursting with sugary sweetness.

No, he wouldn't leave. Maddox might need his help. Hell, who was he kidding? When did the boss man *not* need Tommy's help? And besides, maybe he'd had a good reason for keeping things secret, or at least keeping them secret temporarily. Maybe like he'd said, it was for Tommy's protection. Tommy had once heard somewhere—maybe on a feed program— that you only got a few real friends in life, and maybe that was true. His turfies the Anarchy Boyz qualified, and so did Bea. And, yes, Maddox did too. So, no, Tommy wouldn't bail.

But not bailing and sitting around doing nothing weren't the same thing. Tommy wasn't good at doing nothing for very long, and an hour later his restlessness got the better of him. Gesturing to the wall feed, he pulled up a comms channel. The box flashed green, superimposed over the security feeds.

No leaving the house, no calls: Maddox had left him with those two instructions. Tommy had already disobeyed the first one, and now he was going to defy the second one. He shrugged and made the call.

He'd never been the kind to follow rules.

7
STANDALONE ARCHIVE

"You want me to do what?" Maddox asked reflexively, surprised by what he'd just heard. From his chair he looked up at Nguyen with an uncertain gaze. The agent stood over him, his face fixed in that scornful condescending stare shared by every cop Maddox had ever known. The stink-eyed expression reserved exclusively for criminals like him.

"You heard me," Nguyen said. "You want to walk out of here a free man, you'll play ball and help us crack open this archive."

Maddox sat there, wondering what had happened in the hour since Nguyen had stormed out of this same room. Something had changed. There was something in his demeanor, other than the standard cop stink-eye. Something was annoying him. Then a possible reason struck him.

"Got your arm twisted by Data Crimes, did you?" he asked. Nguyen's reaction told Maddox the guess had been a good one. "They heard you had a real live datajacker in custody, and you didn't want to hand me over." He smirked at Nguyen. "Worried I might let something slip, yeah?"

Nguyen rushed at Maddox and grabbed him by the lapels of his jacket. Rooney's voice popped into Maddox's head.

Shouldn't have smiled at him, boyo.

Nguyen pushed Maddox hard, sending him flailing backwards and out of the chair. The chair back smacked loudly against the floor, and behind Nguyen a guard appeared in the doorway.

"Everything's fine in here," Nguyen said, waving off the guard. "We're all good. Just having a little chat, that's all."

The guard wavered for a moment, then slowly backed away and closed the door, leaving the two alone again.

Nguyen's stare hadn't moved off of Maddox. "You fuck with me, jacker, and it'll be the last thing you ever do."

Maddox sat up and rubbed the back of his head where it had struck the floor. "I believe you." He winced as he found the small knot that had already formed. Whatever happened to the good cop, bad cop routine? he wondered. Nguyen had to be stressing hard to strike out at him like that. Maddox had apparently gotten much further under the agent's skin than he'd reckoned.

"And if I say no?" Maddox asked.

Nguyen crossed his arms. "And why would you do that?"

Maddox motioned to some point beyond the room. "Look, whether you believe it or not, that killer AI's out there right now, hunting me. It doesn't rest, it doesn't sleep, and it's got eyes and ears everywhere, on the street and in virtual space. If I plug in, it'll be

33

like stepping into a spotlight. Maybe it'll take a few minutes to find me, maybe only a few seconds. But the moment it sniffs me out, it's going to hit me with a brain spike or a lethal dose of neuro feedback or some other nasty little weapon. And then that's it, I'm done. So maybe you can understand my hesitation, Agent Nguyen."

"This archive they want you crack," Nguyen said, unmoved by Maddox's words, "they said it was offline. It's a...what do you call it...?" He couldn't seem to find the right term.

"A standalone," Maddox said.

"Yes, a standalone. That means it's never been connected to anything, correct?"

"Yes," Maddox conceded. "That's right."

"Then what's the big worry? If that thing's really after you, it won't see you if you're not plugged into virtual space, am I right?"

There wasn't much point in arguing. Data technology wasn't Nguyen's specialty. Like most people, what he knew about tech was from a user's standpoint. Entertainment feeds and apps in his specs. Beyond that it was all a mystery to him. Dataspheres, automated security bots, and core virtual space were the hidden plumbing behind the walls. For Agent Nguyen, a standalone archive was synonymous with an unbreakable barrier.

But he hadn't seen what Maddox had in the past couple years. And neither had his colleagues in the Data Crimes division. They hadn't witnessed firsthand the impossible feats a superintelligent AI could pull off. A standalone archive inside FBI headquarters was secure. Maybe about as secure a digital environment as he could imagine. But it might not be secure enough.

"It's not that simple," he tried to explain, but the FBI man cut him off.

"Look," Agent Nguyen growled, stepping forward and balling his fists. "I don't care if you pull it off or not, but you're going to give it a try, understand? And then you're going to get the hell out of this facility and never come back."

Looks like that bluff of yours didn't work, boyo.

Tell me something I don't know, Roon.

The voice in his head, he knew, wasn't actually Rooney's ghost. It was a figment of his imagination, a symptom of his own damaged psyche that appeared and disappeared at unpredictable times. Sometimes the voice was a comfort to him, but other times, like now, it was like a nosy eavesdropper. And it was especially annoying when the nosy eavesdropper was right.

Like every good cop, Nguyen was adept at reading body language. He seemed to sense that Maddox's resistance had weakened, and he gave the datajacker an approving nod.

"All right, then," he said. "And keep your mouth shut about Manhattan. Let the past stay in the past where it belongs. We understand each other?"

Maddox sighed in resignation. "We do."

8
CALL FROM D.C.

The limo stopped, the back door opened, and Minister Hanson stepped out. Beatrice muttered a curse under her breath. She hated it when he did this sort of thing. It made her job so much harder.

Gavin Hanson, minister of finance, was no easy body to guard. He was a people person who loved to shake the hands, kiss the cheeks, pat the backs of his Canadian constituency. She'd told him the crowds lining parade routes were impossible to secure, so he should stay in the limo and wave to the crowd from the vehicle's sunroof. But no, he couldn't stick with the plan. Couldn't remain fifty safe feet from the cheering crowd, waving their little red-and-white flags. He had to press some flesh.

"Sir," Beatrice said, moving from her position at the rear of the vehicle to his side. "We hadn't planned for a meet-and-greet."

"You worry too much," Hanson said, buttoning his blazer and already striding toward the crowded walkway.

"I'm sorry, sir," she said firmly, keeping close to

him, "but I'm going to have to ask you to return to the limo."

Minister Hanson didn't break his pace, didn't even glance in her direction, his beaming smile directed at the throng of well-wishers beyond the police barrier. He waved with both hands and told her, "Only be a minute. Photo ops like these don't happen every day."

"Sir, I'm going to have to insist—"

"I'm not listening to you," Hanson said, the cheery smile on his face undiminished, "but if you want to keep your job, you'll listen to me."

Frowning, Beatrice touched the comms bug in her ear. "We're stopping for a minute," she told her crew. "Stay with him."

Jogging over, the four others in the security detail surrounded the minister as he reached the police barrier. They warily scanned the assembled throng, their specs loaded with the latest security apps that picked up on furtive movements, unusual tension in facial expressions, or strange bulges in clothing that could be a concealed weapon. Anything that might reveal a wolf assassin hiding in the pack of citizen sheep.

Beatrice scanned the area, then grunted in disapproval. Midrise buildings all around. Within seconds she counted a dozen excellent vantage points. The minister had stopped the limo in the middle of a sniper's paradise.

The drone! She'd almost forgotten to get it out. Reaching into her jacket pocket, she removed the bumblebee drone and tossed it in the direction of the minister. Tiny rotors popped out of its carapace and it hung in the air for a moment, orienting itself. When its feed appeared in her specs, she tagged the minister and subvocalized a command, instructing the tiny machine to scan the crowd in a five-meter radius around her client. Her extra set of eyes and ears flitted back and forth, two meters above the crowd's heads, as the minister leaned over the police barrier, grasping hand after hand, working the crowd. Tennis-ball-sized drones from various news outlets hovered nearby, recording the moment.

As Minister Hanson worked his way down the line, a man leaped over the police barrier. A rush of adrenaline kicked off her neurochems, a refresher package she'd purchased the prior month, and time dilated into slow motion. Her senses enhanced, she noted a telltale sag in the man's right jacket pocket. A handgun, and he was reaching for it as he rushed toward the minister. With her reflexes boosted, she raised her Ruger and leveled it at the man before his hand had even reached his pocket.

Firing a shot in that instant was problematic, to say the least. If she missed, some bystander in the crowd behind the man would take the bullet.

She fired. She didn't miss.

The man dropped instantly, tumbling to the ground and holding his midsection. The crowd panicked, scattering like ants from a disturbed mound. Screams and shouts filled the air. The security detail instantly converged on the minister with their firearms drawn, forming a protective ring around him.

Beatrice walked over to the downed man. He writhed in pain and blood spurted from his mouth. One of her crew disarmed the man, removing a small-caliber pistol from the man's jacket.

She looked over at Minister Hanson. The politician was white with shock, his mouth hanging open. She shook her head at him.

"Maybe next time you'll listen…sir." She leveled her gun at the would-be assassin and shot him squarely in the forehead.

CALL INCOMING…CALL INCOMING…

White letters flashed in front of her, suspended in the air, large and impossible to ignore. "Okay, okay, I'm coming," she said. "End simulation."

The sniper's paradise disappeared, replaced with a white nothingness all around her. Another shift and she was in her condo again, removing the trodeband from her head and tossing it onto the sofa. Her specs blinked on the end table. She put them on and answered the call.

The worried face of Tommy Park appeared, superimposed on her lens.

"Hey, B," the kid said. "You got a minute?"

* * *

"You've got to be shitting me," Beatrice said minutes later, reeling from the kid's unbelievable story.

"I swear to God," the kid said. "Every word of it's true. We barely made it out of Manny Hatty." Out of Manhattan, Beatrice translated inwardly.

She sat there, trying to make sense of everything the kid had just recounted. But there was no making sense of it. The Latour-Fisher AI, the entity Maddox had destroyed—or thought he had destroyed—was back from the dead? It was back, gone rogue, and it wanted Maddox out of the picture?

"Kid," she said, "how can you be sure?"

"B," the kid said, dead serious, "we're sure, all right?"

"Where are you now?"

"A safe house in D.C."

D.C.? Why had the salaryman taken the kid there? Why hadn't he gotten out of the City altogether?

She blinked up a tracer, geotagged the kid's location, and stored it away.

"Where is he now?" she asked.

"I don't know," Tommy said. "He said he was going to try and get us some help."

"From who?"

"He wouldn't tell me. Said the less I knew the better."

Beatrice snorted. Typical Maddox, keeping things close to his vest. Keeping secrets.

"He probably told you to stay off comms too, didn't he?" she asked.

The kid shrugged. "He might have said something like that. But hell, he's been gone for a whole day. What am I supposed to do, just sit here?"

She couldn't blame him. The salaryman had dumped him with no explanation, no way to contact him, and no clear idea of when he'd return. And the kid wasn't the kind to just sit around on his hands indefinitely.

If what the kid said was accurate, and they really did have that monster of an AI on their tails, then any kind of comms was a big risk, even over an encrypted connection. AIs had ways of finding you. They had tools and methods and programs a hired fist like her couldn't begin to comprehend.

"All right," she said, "listen to me. It's probably not a good idea to stay on this connection too long. Let me take care of a couple things and I'll call you right back."

If her words managed to lessen the kid's anxiety, it

didn't register in his expression. He still looked as worried as when he'd first called her.

"Half an hour at most," she assured him. "I'll call you back. I promise."

Beatrice disconnected, sank back in the sofa cushion, and let out a long breath. Jesus, Mary, and Joseph, what madness! Could it really have come back? Or perhaps some portion of it had survived? And was that even possible? She was no expert on these things. But even if a small part of the AI had survived, Maddox and Tommy would surely be in some very deep shit. And if they were, then she might be in just as deep. She had her own ugly past with the Latour-Fisher AI, not so different from Maddox's. So if the thing was back from the dead, looking for revenge (did AIs even do that?), would it be coming after her too? And if so, why hadn't it found her already? She wasn't exactly hard to track down. Unlike the salaryman, she wasn't living under a false identity, committing crimes and trying to stay under the radar.

Or maybe that whole line of thinking was wrong. AIs weren't sentimental entities, and pinning their reasoning to human emotions and drives was a mistake. They operated on a different level. A level of cold logic, of statistics and probabilities. Anger and fear, joy and sadness: these were never part of an AI's machinations. If the Latour-Fisher entity had really returned, whatever it was up to wasn't about vengeance. More likely, it simply viewed the salaryman as a dangerous, uncontrollable weapon. A weapon its rival had effectively used against it once, and it didn't want there to be a second time. The more she pondered it, the more reasonable this explanation seemed. The Latour-Fisher AI wanted the wild card named Blackburn Maddox removed from the game.

Beatrice clenched her fists. And poor Tommy was stuck in the middle of it again. She cursed herself for not trying to persuade the kid to leave the salaryman's side when she'd last seen him in Manhattan, for not grabbing him by the shirt collar and dragging him out of the City.

And as for Maddox, her feelings were more...complicated. She'd once believed that despite the harrowing times they'd been through together, the crossing paths of their lives had been a good thing. That they'd found something in one another, that unnameable thing you wanted to hold on to and not let go of. But then she'd discovered he'd lied to her, kept important things hidden from her. She'd realized he wasn't the person she'd thought he was. He wasn't someone she could trust. She didn't hate the datajacker, didn't wish him any harm. But she sure as hell wasn't going to stick her neck out for him again.

The kid, though. She couldn't sit here, knowing he was alone and scared and caught in the crossfire. Couldn't leave him to some unknown fate. She had to go and get him.

She made some calls and cashed in a few owed favors. A colleague from her line of business agreed to cover her security gig for the following few days. Then she reached out to the client, who wasn't pleased, to put it mildly, with the late-night call and the sudden replacement. She doubted he'd renew her contract after such an unprofessional move. But whatever. There was always another job around the corner. The world was full of rich assholes who needed protection.

Her business done, she called up flight schedules on her specs. The remaining red-eye flights to the City were fully booked, and there were no charters available this late. She reserved a spot on the next morning's earliest flight, then called Tommy back to tell him she'd be there by ten o'clock tomorrow. He didn't answer. She tried again. Nothing.

Over the next three hours she called every ten minutes. But the kid never answered.

9
HARD LANDING

Half an hour, she'd said. Half an hour, max.

Tommy checked the time on the wall feed again. Only twelve minutes had passed. Jesus, he was making himself crazy. If he only had some games or porn on this thing to distract himself for a while.

Food, he suddenly thought. That would do it. He'd warm up a bit of the veggie stir fry he hadn't tried yet, give it a taste. True, he wasn't really hungry, but the task would help a few minutes pass. He started to move toward the kitchen when an alert on the feed caught his eye.

Something had tripped one of the motion scanners. Then a second scanner beeped, followed by a third. Tommy licked his lips, waiting for the app's recognition algorithm to show him what was out there.

IDENTIFICATION ERROR.

The same words flashed on all three feeds. Tommy wasn't sure what that meant. Was the software glitching? Had something small, like a bee or a moth, flown through the scanners' broadcast cones and confused the ID algos? There was nothing on any of the cams. No movement he could see anywhere.

He turned off the overhead light and moved to a window. The sun had set in the last half hour, and Tommy notched up the light sensitivity on his specs. Keeping his body hidden from view, he peered outside. The scanner he'd placed on the front corner of the patio was still there. Its tiny indicator light, barely visible, blinked green.

From behind him he heard another warning beep. Turning, he gasped at what he saw on the feed. A silhouetted figure crept toward the house, crouched down, a pistol in his hand.

His ears buzzing with a sudden rush of blood, Tommy turned again to the window. Squinting, he spotted the figure's faint outline, ten feet from the front door. The figure's clothing almost, but not quite perfectly, blended in with the surroundings. Adaptive camo, Tommy thought, which explained the ID error. He bolted for the back bedroom as two more warning beeps sounded. Before he hit the hallway, from the corner of his vision he saw two more armed figures on the feeds, creeping toward the house. In the bedroom he yanked heavily on the attic rope, and the overhead trap door yawned open. As he hurriedly unfolded the ladder, the sound of the front door crashing open came from the front of the house. He flew up the ladder as shouting voices filled the space below him. With the blood pounding in his ears, he couldn't make out what they were saying.

Scrambling across the attic's planked floor, he reached the rusted old intake vent he'd noticed on his earlier exploration. He kicked hard, knocking the bottom of the vent free of its housing. The top portion didn't want to give up its hold so easily, but on Tommy's third kick the entire vent flew outward, tumbling across the roof and leaving a gaping hole behind.

"Stop right there!" a voice shouted from below.

Tommy scrambled through the opening. A tight fit, he barely made it through, scraping his shoulders and thighs on the rough edges of what was left of the housing. He fell forward, hitting the roof on his belly. He stood up quickly, clambered to the edge of the roof, and looked down.

"Freeze!" the same voice shouted.

Tommy jumped, landing hard in the neighboring lot. Something in his ankle snapped on impact, and he cried out as he rolled into the brush. He reached down and clutched his foot as pain bloomed through his lower leg. He looked back at the house, squinting in the darkness. A man had tried to follow him but had become stuck halfway through. Tommy patted the ground around him and found his specs. He put them on, looked at the man again. With the ambient light scaled up, he saw the man clearly now but didn't recognize him. Just some old fook with a big mustache, too fat around the middle to follow Tommy through his improvised escape route.

His foot in agony, Tommy rose and limped away as quickly as he could. He still heard the voices behind him, but they grew steadily softer and farther away. He hobbled down the alleyway, a path with overgrowth so thick and tall that at times he had to move it aside with his hands. It was slow going, but the dense brush made for good cover. He tried to keep as much weight off his injured foot as possible, but even the lightest touch of his toe to the ground felt like someone driving a nail through the bottom of his heel. Head down, he kept moving, limping along and clearing a path through the tangle of weeds and wild grass.

Suddenly he was out of it, stumbling into a dark, deserted street lined with empty lots. He looked around. Where to go now? Or should he hide and wait? Then a thought struck him.

Beatrice! He had to reach her, had to let her what was happening. As he blinked up her number, he felt a sharp jab in his chest. He looked down.

What looked like a small dart had pierced through his shirt and was stuck in his belly. The thing felt like a bee sting, and its needle tip had pierced a centimeter deep into his skin.

"Oh shit," Tommy said, recognizing what it was. He looked up, searching the darkness for the shooter. Five meters away a man crouched on one knee, his taser pistol drawn and pointed at Tommy. The man thumbed a switch on the weapon and Tommy's entire body went rigid with a surge of electricity. He collapsed to the ground, writhing in pain.

10
KIPLING'S TASK

"Hope you got some rest, jacker," Nguyen said. "You've got a big day ahead of you." He sipped coffee from a disposable cup.

They stood shoulder to shoulder in the hotel elevator. Nguyen pressed the lobby button and the doors slid shut. The hotel they'd put Maddox up in for the night catered to traveling executive types. He'd slept in a spacious suite on a comfortable bed, and the New York strip he'd ordered from room service—courtesy of the FBI—had been the best meal he'd had in a long while. Under other circumstances, it would have been an enjoyable stay. But there were two armed guards stationed inside the room with him, watching his every move. And he couldn't stop thinking about Tommy, who he hadn't expected to leave alone for more than a few hours.

The elevator car descended. He wondered what kind of night the kid had spent, alone in the safe house. It had been over a full day since he'd left the kid alone. By now he'd be worried, probably starting to wonder if Maddox would return at all. And no doubt he was starving too. Tommy's adolescent appetite needed a near-constant supply of calories, usually in the form of Thai food. Maddox knew if the kid hadn't already ventured out for something to eat, then he would soon. The kid was smart, though. He knew how to keep his head down, knew how to keep from being IDed.

Still, with each passing hour, the kid's hope would ebb away a bit more, and eventually his nerves would get the better of him. Tommy was far from the impulsive youth Maddox had first met nearly two years ago, but he was still a kid. He still had his moments of questionable teenage judgment. Maddox knew he couldn't leave the kid on his own for too long.

"I need you to make a call for me," he said. "Before I try to crack this archive."

Nguyen gave him a sidelong glance. "I'm not your call app, jacker."

"It's important," Maddox said. "I just want someone to know I'm all right."

The agent lifted an eyebrow. "You're pretty far from all right, the way I see it."

"'All right' meaning not in jail," he amended.

"After," he said, then adding with a scoffing tone, "after you perform this techie miracle."

Maddox found himself annoyed at the man's skepticism. A datajacker's ego bruises easily, Rooney had once told him. "Don't think I can do it?"

The agent drank his coffee. "I'll tell you what I think." He turned to him, fixed him with a harsh stare. "I think you're a criminal who'll say or do anything to get out of whatever mess you're in. And I think you're playing a dangerous game. And I think if it were up to me, last night you would have slept on a jail cell floor instead of in a four-star hotel."

Maddox said nothing, recalling the first thing Rooney had taught him about dealing with angry cops: it's best to keep your mouth shut around them.

Roon's advice felt especially true at the moment.

*   *   *

A short ground car ride and three security checkpoints later, Maddox and Agent Nguyen stepped out of another elevator onto the tenth floor of the FBI building. As they moved along the corridor, Maddox flashed back to his brief tenure in the corporate world. The place where he'd worked hadn't been terribly different from where he found himself now. Tighter security here, of course, but aside from that, the two settings had much in common. Smartly dressed, busy people with coffees in hand strode purposefully through the lobby and along the hallways. Small knots of coworkers here and there made small talk. Executive suites, meeting rooms, a half-eaten box of donuts lying open on a workstation.

The legit world, he reflected. The normal world. Where you walked the straight and narrow, followed all the rules. You paid your taxes and did what you were told. You played the game the way the higher-ups expected you to. You never questioned, never made waves.

He'd never felt comfortable in the legit world. Sure, he'd earned well, and he'd had a comfortable life, free from the worries of a datajacker's lawless existence. But he'd eventually seen the straight life for what it was: a cage. A nice cage, granted. A cage far removed from the constant scramble of the City's floor. A cage with the best food and the hottest women and very comfortable furniture. But a cage all the same.

Passing through a doorway, Maddox and Nguyen had apparently reached their destination.

"He's all yours," Nguyen announced, finally releasing his grip on Maddox's arm.

Nguyen's colleague, a short heavyset man of around fifty, nodded. "Thank you, Agent Nguyen." The man wore a simple pair of midrange wire-framed specs.

"Mind if I stay and watch?" Nguyen asked.

"By all means," the man said, disappointing Maddox, who'd hoped to be free of his less-than-hospitable minder. "Though I'll have to warn you, it's pretty tedious stuff. Not exactly a spectator sport, so to speak."

"That's all right," Nguyen said, casting a quick glance at Maddox. "I'd like to see how this turns out."

The man smiled politely. "You're more than welcome to stay." Then the man rubbed his hands together. "All right, then. Let's get started, shall we?"

Introducing himself to Maddox as Stellan Kipling, director of Data Crimes, he shook Maddox's hand and smiled warmly. "My apologies for making you wait overnight for me," Kipling said. "I was out of town until quite late yesterday. How were the accommodations?"

"They were fine," Maddox said, glancing briefly at Nguyen. "Better than I expected."

"Excellent."

Kipling didn't strike Maddox as someone who worked in law enforcement. He seemed less like a cop than some disheveled scientist. The knot on his tie was lopsided, his cheap suit was in desperate need of a press, and atop his head was a messy, comically thin comb-over.

"I do hope you can help us," Kipling said. "I've never seen a harder nut to crack than this pesky little archive. It's been giving us fits around here for weeks." He looked over at Nguyen. "I'll have someone come for you once we get started, Agent. But first I'd like to review a few things with Mr. Maddox. Shop talk, you understand."

Nguyen's expression soured at the dismissal. "Yes, sir," he said after a moment. Maddox smiled inwardly, taking no small amount of satisfaction in the agent's disappointment.

Kipling led Maddox to a meeting room, a larger version of the space where Maddox had been detained the day before. Several chairs were pushed under a long rectangular table, and a standby icon hovered a few inches above the tabletop's center. Kipling closed the door behind him, leaving the two alone in the room.

"Sit," Kipling said, motioning. Maddox sat and Kipling took a seat across the table from him. The director folded his hands on the table. "Now," he said, lifting his chin, "tell me what you need."

Maddox furrowed his brow. "But I don't even know what kind of archive it is."

Kipling straightened his back. "Of course you don't," he said. "My apologies." He turned his head away from Maddox and spoke to someone through his specs. "Can you please bring the diamond to conference room B?"

"Diamond?" Maddox asked.

"Yes," Kipling said. "As in impossible to break.

It's the nickname my staff has given the damned thing." Then he frowned and muttered, "'Stone in my shoe' would have been a more appropriate moniker, if you ask me."

Behind the director, the door opened. A young woman wearing white gloves carried a small standalone archive, roughly four inches square. She gingerly placed it in front of Kipling.

"Thank you, Darla," he said. After the woman left the room, Kipling slid the archive across the table. "Go ahead, take a look."

Maddox picked up the little black cube, turned it over in his hands. "What you're looking at there," Kipling said, "is an entirely unique archive, as far as we can tell. It appears to have been a one-off manufacture, with its own physical and cybernetic architecture."

Maddox nodded. "A black hole," he said.

Kipling lifted his chin. "Ah, yes. That's what you dataja...what those in your profession call them, isn't it?"

Maddox chuckled inwardly. The man had nearly called him a datajacker. In Kipling's world, and especially inside the walls of this building, calling someone a datajacker was like calling them a pimp or a narco. It was a dirty accusation, an insult.

"They're pretty costly to make," Maddox said.

"The owner had no shortage of funds," Kipling said.

One-off archives, or black holes, were designed and fabricated by experts from the ground up, and no two were alike. At a minimum, you needed a hardware architect, an encryption engineer, and at least a couple ops system designers. And you couldn't just grab some data system student right out of college. You needed experienced talent if you wanted to make a one-of-a-kind breach-proof archive. He'd dabbled in their manufacture from time to time, mostly on the encryption side. His datajacking clients—for obvious reasons—often needed an offline archive with impenetrable crypto.

"Who did this one belong to?" Maddox asked.

"I'm afraid I can't tell you that," Kipling replied.

"What can you tell me, then?" Maddox placed the little cube back on the tabletop.

"I can tell you every cryptography expert we have on-site couldn't put as much as a scratch on this thing, metaphorically speaking. So we brought in data security consultants from the private sector. Best in the business. They couldn't make heads or tails of it either."

"What about your AIs?" Maddox asked.

"They fared no better, unfortunately," Kipling said, then grunted. "If you only knew how many headaches this little…thing has caused." He stared at the archive like he wanted to pick it up and throw it out the window.

None of what Maddox had heard in the last few minutes raised his spirits. Pretty much the opposite, in fact. If crypto gurus and AIs had already taken their best shots at cracking the thing open, what chance would he have? This Kipling fellow was just rolling the dice, hoping against hope some random datajacker could break the archive's crypto out of sheer luck.

Every heard the phrase "snowball's chance in hell," boyo?

Not funny, Roon.

Pushing away the voice in his head, Maddox took

a breath. "All right," he said, "here's what I need."

He made a list, calling off item after item as Kipling nodded and blinked, logging the requested gear in his specs. It was the wish list of all wish lists, because why the hell not? The latest trode and deck set from Tani-Nakashima, a high-end suite of apps, most of which he wouldn't need, and the best anti-crypto tools you could find on the legit market.

When Maddox finished, the director grinned. "And would you like fries with that?"

Maddox chuckled inwardly as Kipling made a call in his specs to some underling, recounting the list and asking them to fetch the gear. Under different circumstances, he might have liked the odd little man. But then he reminded himself where he was and what was about to happen. Within the hour, he'd almost certainly fail at the impossible task he'd been given. And when that happened, Nguyen would toss him back out onto the street. Then that thing would come after him again. And sooner or later, it would find him.

Bringing Tommy to D.C. had been a mistake, Maddox admitted, cursing himself inwardly for making such a stupid blunder. Had he been thinking more clearly at the time, he would have left the kid in Manhattan. Or left him by the side of the road on the way to D.C. The farther away from this bad-luck datajacker, the better.

Because when it came right down to it, Maddox was toxic. Not only now, he reflected, but always. Anyone who got close to him eventually paid dearly for it. Rooney and Maddox's friend Jack were dead because of him. And then there was Beatrice and Tommy and the kid's biker friends. They'd each come within inches of suffering the same fate. All because of their unfortunate acquaintance with one Blackburn Maddox.

But no more, he promised himself. If by some miracle he lived longer than the next day or two, he'd take steps to sever those connections permanently. He'd leave the country, change his name, alter his face. Whatever it took to vanish from Bea's and Tommy's lives completely, to spare them from the curse of knowing him, he was determined to do it.

"Anything else?" Kipling asked, snapping Maddox out of his thoughts.

The datajacker blew out a breath. "No, that should be plenty."

Within ten minutes the woman who'd brought the archive entered the room again, laying every piece of gear Maddox had requested on the table in front of him. Impressed, the datajacker nodded. "That didn't take long."

The director grinned, taking something from the woman as she left. "We aim to please." He set the object atop the table and slid it over to Maddox. A ceramic ashtray emblazoned with the FBI logo. Damn, Maddox thought. This Kipling didn't miss a thing.

"Now," the director said, "let's see what you can do, shall we?"

*   *   *

The trodeband securely fastened to his head, Maddox reminded himself the gear was offline. The deck and trode set lying in front of him, physically tethered to the archive by a cable, had no connection to the vast cybernetic universe of virtual space. And similar to the one-off archive, the VS deck's connectivity was disabled. So when he plugged in, he'd be on an island in the middle of a boundless sea. Unseen and untouchable.

Still, as he fired up the deck, he felt a nervous twitch in his stomach. He tried to calm his mind, tried not to think about the thing hunting him.

Above the table, a standby icon floated on the holo monitor, slowly rotating. Kipling would watch Maddox's progress, much in the same way his old corporati colleagues used to watch him chase down would-be datajackers. Beyond the room's window, Agent Nguyen stood in the hallway, his arms crossed and eyes locked on Maddox.

Maddox blew out a breath. Might as well get it over with. "All right, I'm plugging in," he told Kipling.

The room around him dissolved into nothingness. His anxiety from a moment before melted away as the silent darkness welcomed him. Here, in the familiar comfort of the digital ether, he was in his element. Here there was no FBI higher-up sitting across from him. No Agent Nguyen staring him down. Only a soothing cybernetic void. He let his body, his meat sack, float away, allowing himself to sink deeply into the standalone construct.

In the next moment, a matrix appeared around him. A kind of room, or rather, the suggestion of a room. A pale green box surrounded him, open at one side. He gazed downward at his digital self, finding a perfectly rendered replica of his body and hands. Right down to the swirls of his fingerprints. Very high-end gear, indeed.

Just beyond the room's open side, the one-off archive slowly materialized, visualizing as a large cube covered in a fine white mist. Maddox stepped forward, watching the swirling patterns of the archive's outermost encryption layer. As he moved closer, he detected a faint hissing. Recognizing the sound, he stopped dead in his tracks. Quickly pulling up a scanner, he sampled the algorithm's patterns, running them through a reverse-compiler.

Unbelievable, he thought as he read the scan's results. This was flat-out unbelievable.

11
CHARTER FLIGHT

Flying private charter. It wasn't cheap, Beatrice reflected, but it was a very nice way to travel. The best way, actually, aside from having your own jet. Charters had excellent food, attentive staff, and comfortable furniture. They were clean and smelled of lavender air freshener, and the restrooms had room to move around in, not like the narrow closets that reeked of crap you found on commercial flights. She treated herself to charters every so often, when the mood struck to spoil herself with a bit of luxury.

When she'd booked this one, however, it had been more out of necessity than self-indulgence. An hour earlier her commercial flight to D.C. had been canceled at the last minute. Desperate to get to D.C. as soon as possible—she hadn't been able to reach Tommy after their one brief call—she'd checked the airport's charter rideshare app in her specs. Luckily, a flight headed to D.C. and scheduled to depart within the next ninety minutes had been looking for another passenger.

The Cessna had twelve seats, but only hers and

two others were occupied. She'd given both her fellow passengers a friendly nod as she'd entered the plane and fastened herself into her seat. After takeoff, the flight attendant served her a ginger ale and an egg white omelet with freshly chopped scallions. When Beatrice finished her breakfast, the attendant removed the plate, and Beatrice turned to the window and stared out at the cloudless blue sky.

She hoped the kid was all right. If she found him—no, *when* she found him—she'd talk some sense into him. Talk him into getting out of the City and coming back with her to Toronto, where she could keep him out of trouble. And when she got away from the City, she could guide him into finding a better way to make a living than the suicidal path that was datajacking.

"Going to D.C. on business?"

Across the aisle and one row back, a fortyish corporati with slicked-back hair gazed at her.

"Yes," she said.

"Same here."

She blinked, darkening her specs, then turned back to the window.

"What kind of business are you in?" he asked.

Mr. McChatty wasn't good at taking hints. Or he simply ignored them. Corporati were like that, more often than not. The highfloor wealthy were accustomed to being listened to by most everyone around them, morning to night. By ass-kissing underlings at the office, who hung on their every word. By maids and nannies and chauffeurs outside the office, whose livelihoods depended on staying in their benefactor's good graces. The notion that someone didn't want to hear the very important things they had to say was unthinkable. At a certain level of self-absorption, one became blind to social cues.

Was she being ungenerous to McChatty? Maybe he was simply the friendly type. No, she reconsidered, taking a second look at him. Probably not. He gave her a rich slimeball kind of vibe, and in her experience, that kind of first impression was rarely wrong.

"Security," she answered, hoping this would turn him off. A fair share of men were intimidated by women who worked in security. McChatty, unfortunately, didn't seem to be among them.

"Excellent," he said, moving up a row, seating himself directly across the aisle.

Briefly, Beatrice glanced back at the charter's only other passenger, seated three rows back. A well-dressed woman roughly Beatrice's own age. The woman gave her a look that was at once sympathetic and slightly amused. Sorry, but better you than me, the woman's expression seemed to say.

"So do you work with a particular company or venue or what?" Ice tinkled in his glass as he absently swirled the scotch or whiskey or whatever it was he was drinking. Beatrice frowned at the man's breakfast selection.

"Private contracts, mostly," she said, then tapped her specs. "I'm sorry, but I need to review a couple contracts."

Hint number two was ignored like the first one had been. "Corporate gigs?" he prodded. "Bodyguard work, stuff like that?" He looked her up and down, giving her a carnal grin. "I can see that. You look like you can handle yourself."

Beatrice sighed. Even the best way to travel had its downsides. Wealthy entitled men: was there anything more annoying? "Look," she said, "I don't mean to be rude, but I really need to get some work done."

The man furrowed his brow. "All right, then," he said dismissively, finishing his drink in a single swallow. If he followed the normal behavior pattern of his kind, next he would either order another drink or grumble something about her being a lesbian. Possibly both.

He held up his empty glass and tapped the side of it. "Another drink over here," he called to the flight attendant.

It wasn't a long flight. A little over an hour. But as the flight attendant arrived with a fresh drink for McChatty, Beatrice knew it was going to feel like much longer. She turned away from the man and pretended to read something in her specs.

"Oh my gosh," the attendant said, "I'm so sorry."

Beatrice looked to find McChatty with a wet crotch and a furious expression. "You clumsy bitch!" he shouted, jumping up out of his seat, frantically wiping the front of his trousers.

"I'm terribly sorry, sir," the attendant said. "Let me get a towel for you."

A smile touched Beatrice's lips. Nothing like a little instant karma—

A horizontal blur flashed across her vision as something dropped over her face. Her head yanked backwards, slamming against the headrest, and her neck constricted violently. Taken completely by surprise, it took a moment for her to realize she was being attacked, choked from behind with a cord or a wire. The attendant and McChatty were instantly on top of her, holding down her arms and legs. The whole thing had been a show, she realized, gagging reflexively and struggling in vain to free her pinned-down limbs. A distraction to throw her off guard so they could ambush her. But who? How?

The edges of her vision went dark as she began to black out.

12
BRAIN SPIKE

Inside the offline construct, Maddox opened a comms window. "I need some assurances," he said to Kipling's floating head.

"Excuse me?" the director asked.

"We haven't agreed to terms yet," Maddox clarified. "I'd like that all squared away before I get started."

Kipling cleared his throat impatiently. "It was my understanding Agent Nguyen already went over this with you. If you manage to retrieve the contents of the archive, intact, you're free to go."

"If it's not too much to ask," Maddox said, "I'd also like your take on a little problem I have. It's the reason I came to see Nguyen, and I'm sure you'll find it interesting." Maddox couldn't see the agent's reaction, but he was certain the temperature of Nguyen's stare had just shot up a couple hundred degrees.

"Ah," Kipling said, apparently intrigued. "The mystery behind your unlawful entry to this facility. I haven't had time to review this with Agent Nguyen.

Yes, yes, of course. In fact, I can't wait to hear it. You must have had a compelling reason to do something so drastic." Chuckling, he added, "Assuming you're not mentally deranged, of course. But provided it doesn't run up against my next meeting, I'll be happy to hear you out. Busy day, you understand."

"It won't take long," Maddox said. "And thanks."

Back in the room, he felt his hands begin a complex series of gestures, movements synced with a succession of subvocalized commands. It was a sequence he thought he'd forgotten, but as he began, it all came back to him.

Like riding a bike, isn't it, boyo?

While juggling chainsaws, he added. Blindfolded.

Seconds later, the mist surrounding the archive faded and disappeared. Maddox glanced over at the still-open comms window, finding the director's eyes wide in disbelief.

The datajacker subvocalized another command, and the front of the archive yawned open before him, revealing its contents. The stored data visualized as a rotating carousel of multicolored cards. The colors represented different logical partitions, Maddox assumed. That was typically how private archives were set up, allowing the owner easy access to the contents.

"How did you…?" Kipling gasped, too stunned to finish the sentence.

"A good magician never reveals his secrets," Maddox said cryptically. He gestured to transfer the data over to his deck. The retrieval process began, visualizing as a rainbow of cards flying out of the archive toward him. A counter appeared, logging the extraction. The slow-moving indicator told Maddox it would take two or three minutes to finish carving out everything. For it to take that long, the archive had to be holding a huge amount of data.

"I'm amazed," Kipling said, his voice full of wonder. "Astounded." What Maddox had done, though, was neither amazing nor astounding. It hadn't even been terribly difficult.

Because he'd designed the encryption himself.

Years ago, he'd helped put together a one-off archive for some up-and-coming crime boss. He couldn't recall the man's name, but he remembered the keyhole sequence he'd hidden within the encryption algorithms. A way to get in no one else knew about. His own secret doorway, invisible to anyone but him.

He'd embedded it on a whim. As an inside joke to himself, perhaps. Or maybe he'd done it just to see if he could. In any case, he'd never thought he'd actually use it. Never thought he'd ever see the archive again, for that matter.

But luck and happenstance were part of every datajacker's existence. And luck—nothing but sheer dumb luck—had brought him and this little archive together again. What a world.

Then something shot out of the archive and hit him, hard. Back in the room his body went rigid, and inside the construct he felt as if his mind had been placed in a vise. There'd been zero warning, zero indication. When he'd peered into the archive seconds earlier, his readout had told him there was nothing inside other than static data.

He tried to gesture, but his hands were useless. His meat sack was frozen in a block of ice as a million nails hammered into his consciousness. It had to be a brain spike of some kind. Buried by the data designer deep inside the archive's innards, cloaked and hidden like a coiled cobra, waiting to strike out at anyone who got too close.

Reality slammed in around him with the sudden violence of a car crash. He was cold, painfully cold. The conference room came into focus. Kipling was next to him, standing impossibly sideways, defying gravity for a brief instant until Maddox oriented himself, realizing it was his own point of view that was off-kilter. He'd collapsed in the chair, and now he was hunched over the table, his head wrenched to one side. Kipling had acted quickly, pulling off the trodeband as soon as Maddox had gone into distress. Now, seeing Maddox still unable to move, the director gingerly removed the deck from under the datajacker, where it had been wedged painfully beneath his chest. Maddox heaved in convulsively and let out a deep breath.

"Can you hear me?" the director asked, grasping his shoulder. "Maddox?"

Slowly, the cold subsided and Maddox began to regain control of his body. He wiggled his fingers, then raised himself up with shaky, weak arms. His mind, thankfully, felt intact. He knew who he was: Blackburn Maddox. He knew where he was: FBI headquarters. And he knew his condition: indefinitely detained.

* * *

One coffee and two cigarettes later, Maddox had somewhat recovered. His hands were still trembling, and he had a pounding headache.

"Thanks for pulling me out," he said.

"Thanks for not dying on me," Kipling replied.

Nguyen had joined them in the room. The three sat around the conference table.

"Did you get what you needed?" Maddox asked, blowing smoke. He reached for the ashtray and rubbed out his cigarette.

"We only recovered about half of the data," Kipling replied. "The other half self-destructed. Irreversibly so, it seems." Before Maddox could register disappointment, the director added, "But what we retained looks quite promising. And certainly enough for the prosecutor's needs."

Nguyen remained silent, but he looked let down by the higher-up's words. If Maddox had felt any better, he would have needled the long-faced agent with a smug grin.

"A keyhole, yes?" Kipling asked. "That's how you cracked it so easily. You knew the encryption engineer, I take it. One of your partners in crime, perhaps?"

Cat's out of the bag, boyo.

"Maybe I'm just that good," Maddox said, ignoring the voice in his head.

"Yes, that's possible," Kipling conceded, "but perhaps not as likely." The director waved his hand dismissively. "But let's put that aside for the moment. You came through for the Bureau, and for that you have my thanks. Now I'd like to live up to my side of the bargain and hear why you came to see our Agent Nguyen yesterday. If you're feeling up to it, that is."

Maddox glanced over at Nguyen. His stony expression betrayed nothing.

"I was hoping he could help me," Maddox said.

"Help you with what?" Kipling asked.

"With…someone I was having problems with."

Maddox took another glance at Nguyen. Gone was the stone-faced gaze from moments before. A furious stare now bore down on Maddox, so hot he could feel it.

"And who exactly was that?" the director pressed, adjusting his specs. "Tell me."

Maddox lit a cigarette, wondering if Kipling's specs had some state-of-the-art lie detector app. Something that caught the smallest telltale waver in your voice or the tiniest surge of skin temperature on your face.

He blew smoke and prepared himself to be laughed at again. "A rogue AI was trying to kill me. *Is* trying to kill me, actually."

Surprisingly, the director didn't burst out in laughter. He only nodded slightly and said, "I see. And why did you reach out to Nguyen for help? Of all people, I mean? He has no expertise in this area."

Nguyen looked as if he wanted to leap across the table and choke the datajacker. Maddox drew on his cigarette, considering his words carefully.

"He worked a bombing case in Manhattan I was…briefly detained on."

"Yes," Kipling said, "I read over your file this morning. Ugly business, that bombing. Good to know you weren't responsible."

"I figured since he knew my name and my background," Maddox explained, "he might believe me and pass me along to the right people."

Moving only his eyes, Kipling glanced briefly over at Nguyen. "And did he believe you?"

Maddox blew smoke. "He had a doubt or two." Understatement of the century, he added inwardly.

"Is that accurate?" Kipling asked, turning to

Nguyen.

The agent blinked, letting the heat drain from his face. "The Bureau's been getting tips on this kind of thing for years, sir. Nothing's ever come of one."

"That's correct," Kipling said. Then he gazed ponderously at Maddox. "But suppose we finally came across one that might have some merit?"

Nguyen leaned forward. "Sir, you can't possibly believe this data—"

"Agent Nguyen," Kipling interrupted, "the man sitting in this room with us has no criminal record, yet we all know what he does for a living. Someone who operates with that kind of caution, with that kind of deliberate prudence, hardly fits the profile of our typical lunatic raving about unchained AIs running amok and secret societies and who knows what else. And he's clearly a top professional in his field, as you just witnessed. That archive's encryption—the one that's confounded every expert we could throw at it—he obviously authored it. That or he was deeply involved in developing it."

Maddox began to speak, but Kipling cut him off with a wave. "Please, don't insult my intelligence by denying it. I've been around encryption cracking since before you were born, Mr. Maddox. I can tell when a safecracker already knows a lock's combination."

Kipling shifted his gaze between Nguyen and Maddox, seemingly amused by their stunned expressions. He folded his hands and placed them atop the table.

"Now," he said to Maddox, "I'd like to hear more about you and this rogue AI." He adjusted his specs. "And, please, don't leave out any details. I want to know everything."

13
GHOST HUNTER

As Kipling had requested, Maddox didn't leave anything out, with a couple exceptions. The first missing portion of his otherwise complete disclosure was Nguyen's compromising history in Manhattan. Now that Maddox had found what appeared to be a receptive audience in Kipling, there seemed little point in poking that particular hornet's nest a second time. He'd also left out his recent visit to Lora's place, letting Kipling assume his ex's location, like those of all the other 'Nettes, had long since been lost to him. He saw no need to drag Lora into his troubles again.

The brain dump took over an hour. There were lots of starts and stops as Kipling interrupted every few minutes, asking questions. Sometimes Maddox had an answer, sometimes he didn't. Nguyen, seated next to the director, said nothing during the entire session, but the more Maddox spoke, the more uncomfortable and agitated Nguyen appeared, though he did his best to mask it from his superior. The datajacker was a threat to his career. A loose cannon who knew damnable secrets from his past. At the moment, with Kipling present, Maddox couldn't tell him not to worry, couldn't assure the agitated agent his secrets were safe. Maybe later, if they were left alone and unmonitored, he'd have the opportunity to allay Agent Nguyen's worries.

Maddox recounted his dealings with the two AIs in detail, relating everything he could recall. What he knew about the Latour-Fisher AI, how he'd discovered the entity had secretly manipulated his life for years, killing his mentor Rooney in the process. How later it had recruited him through a company talent scout, seducing him with a cushy corporate job, a decent salary, and a roomy condo high above the City's congested valley floor. A gilded cage of an existence, far removed from a datajacker's hustling street life. A peaceful life he'd admittedly enjoyed. A life he might have never abandoned if he hadn't accidentally discovered the truth behind the entity's manipulation, how for years Maddox had unknowingly played a part in a secret war being waged between opposing AIs.

A surge of the old anger hit him as he spoke, the rage he'd felt when he'd first pieced it all together, confirming the horrible truth. When he'd realized a superintelligent machine had played him for a fool. The guilt was there too. Unlike the anger, though, which could come and go like bad weather, the guilt never really went away. He'd felt it yesterday and he'd felt it this morning. Come tomorrow, it would be there still, as heavy and inescapable as ever.

There'd been a period when he'd attempted to get past it, to heal himself. Back when he'd been living the good life as a salaryman, he'd sometimes try to tell himself it hadn't been his fault, but something inside him had never bought into that. After all, if Rooney had never met him, never made the fatal mistake of taking him in, the old man would still be alive somewhere in the City, jacking data and getting by.

"You were saying?" Kipling prompted him.

Maddox snapped his attention back to the present. Distracted by his own haunting thoughts, he hadn't realized he'd stopped talking.

He went on. Kipling listened attentively, nodding as Maddox shifted the narrative to his history with the other AI, the unnamed rogue that had presented itself through a grandmotherly avatar on a virtual beach. Maddox had first learned of her...of *its* existence through Lora, his ex-lover who'd joined the AI's underground movement, the secret cult of urban legend whose adherents had illegal brainjacks drilled into their heads. The banned mods gave the nameless AI direct and unfettered access to the minds of its followers. To help them make better decisions. To guide them through their optimal life journey. That was the pitch, anyway. And Lora had bought into it, along with thousands of other true believers around the world.

Kipling seemed particularly interested in the 'Nettes and their founder AI. Unlike Nguyen, who'd laughed at Maddox as if he'd just claimed to have seen a dinosaur walking down Fifth Avenue, the director narrowed his eyes listened with a keen, almost childlike fascination.

Finally, Maddox reached the end of his story, describing his touch-and-go moments in Manhattan two days earlier, the nightmarish events still fresh in his mind. The Latour-Fisher AI had hijacked dozens of bots and hovers, turning them into bombs and missiles.

"Then I drove here and dropped in on Agent Nguyen," Maddox said. "The rest of it you know already."

He removed the tobacco bag from his pocket and began to roll a cigarette. For a long moment no one spoke.

"May I ask you something?" Kipling finally said.

Maddox lit the tip and inhaled. "Sure."

"Why do you roll your own cigarettes?" he asked.

Of all the questions the director could have asked at that moment, this might have been the one Maddox least expected.

"Smoking's bad for your health. And I've found if I roll my own, I smoke a lot less." The statement was true, but not entirely. Maddox had no intention of sharing the full, very personal truth. Years ago, when Rooney, an ex-smoker himself, had failed to convince his apprentice to kick the habit, he'd taught the twenty-five-year-old Maddox how to roll cigarettes, hoping this would at least reduce his pack-a-day habit to a less harmful level. The ploy had worked. And ever since Rooney's death, each time Maddox rolled a cigarette, it felt like a nod to the old man's memory. A little memorial of sorts.

"I see," Kipling said. Then he stood up. "Agent Nguyen, would you excuse us for a moment?"

Reluctantly, Nguyen rose from his chair and left the conference room. When the door closed behind him, Kipling said, "That's only a partial truth, isn't it? There's another reason you roll your cigarettes. A more important reason, I suspect."

Maddox swallowed. "You might be right about that."

The director tapped his specs. "You'd be amazed how accurate this application is. It picks up on the slightest deception or attempted misdirection. It's still in beta testing, but so far I've found it to be amazingly accurate."

So Maddox had guessed right earlier. The man had some kind of lie detector app running. "I'd love to see it sometime."

Kipling shook his head politely. "I'm afraid it's limited to senior Bureau staff at the moment. Not even your good friend Agent Nguyen has access yet. Though I'm sure before long you'll be able to find it somewhere on your black market. It seems like everything we come up with ends up there sooner or later."

"Then you know I'm not lying about all this," Maddox said.

"That, or you're the most capable liar I've ever come across." He quickly added, "I don't believe you're lying, for the record."

"You don't?"

Kipling sat back down. "Don't get me wrong, Mr. Maddox. Believing you're not lying and believing everything you've just related is true are two very different things. You might believe with every fiber of your being that I'm an alien in disguise, but that wouldn't make it true, would it?" He tapped his specs a second time. "And it wouldn't register as a deception in these either."

Maddox frowned and blew smoke. "So I may not be a liar, but I might be crazy. Is that it?"

The director chuckled. "I don't believe you're crazy either. But I have to tell you, this is one whopper of a tale you've laid out for me this morning.

If I believed every word of it with no evidence to back it up, I wouldn't be much of an investigator, would I?"

"I suppose not." Maddox couldn't blame the man. It was a hell of a lot to take in. Still, he sensed there had been something Kipling had latched onto, something about the 'Nettes that had piqued his interest.

Kipling removed his specs and laid them on the table. "This information you said you acquired about the 'Nettes, the comprehensive list of their names and locations. Do you still have it?"

"Not on me," Maddox replied. "It's on a needle archive in my apartment. But it's useless now."

"How so?" Kipling asked.

Maddox explained that as far as he could tell, every last 'Nette had assumed a new identity. When Maddox had managed to steal the names and residences of every living 'Nette, compromising the movement's secrecy, the cult's AI leader had acted swiftly, erasing every trace of its followers' previous lives. Birth records, Social Security numbers, job histories. All of it, gone. Tens of thousands of people had effectively vanished from society and soon thereafter reappeared in some new life with a new name and new personal history, finding new jobs and settling into new living arrangements. The information Maddox had stolen, the identities of their former selves, had long since become a meaningless list of names and addresses.

Kipling narrowed his eyes. "Do you happen to remember how many of these 'Nettes, as you call them, were located in the New York area?"

As it happened, Maddox had retained this tidbit of

information. "A bit over ten thousand."

Kipling snapped his fingers. "Exactly the number I'd hoped for, give or take a thousand."

"I'm not following you," Maddox said, blowing smoke.

"Let me show you something." The director gestured up the table's inbuilt holo display. After a couple hand movements and murmured voice commands, a line graph appeared, floating half a meter above the table.

"This is the number of No-ID missing persons cases per month over the last year," Kipling explained, "for the greater New York area."

"No-ID?" Maddox asked.

"Meaning the authorities could find no records of the person reported missing. For example, suppose I reported my next-door neighbor, John Smith, who lives on 123 Maple Avenue, as missing, but the police could find no record of a Mr. Smith ever having lived there. Or any record of Mr. Smith's having ever existed, for that matter. This kind of case would be tagged with a No-ID label."

"That can't happen very often," Maddox said.

"It doesn't, and that's precisely my point. Typically it's some mentally unbalanced person spinning a story or someone misremembering a name, and as you point out, these kinds of cases are few and far between. Maybe a handful per day on average, and this is for all of New York, mind you." He leaned forward and ran his finger over the large spike in the center of the graph. "But look here. This is ten thousand, four hundred and sixty-two No-ID missing persons cases over two calendar months."

Smiling with satisfaction, Kipling crossed his arms.

"I believe these are your 'Nettes, Mr. Maddox. And the information on your archive, the quantities it contains, could go a long way in substantiating it."

"So you do believe me, then," Maddox said.

"I'm not sure I'd go quite that far. Not yet, at least. Let's just say I'm not inclined to disbelieve you. At least on this particular point."

Maddox flicked the cigarette over the ashtray. It might not have been full vindication, he mused, but it was a hell of a lot better than being laughed at and handcuffed.

"This is the sort of thing," Kipling said, "is what I like to refer to as a *fingerprint*."

"An AI's fingerprint," Maddox said.

"Exactly." He sat down again, this time in the chair next to Maddox. "You see, occasionally we see strange anomalies in our data universe. Trends we can't explain, like this one." He motioned to the floating graph. "More often, it's some strange occurrence in virtual space. A datasphere collapse with no known cause. Or perhaps the appearance of a bottleneck in an entire nation's information flow, there and gone so quickly no one can determine how it happened. I've collected dozens of these phenomena over the years, and I believe they're fingerprints of a sort. Evidence that points to the existence of an unconstrained artificial intelligence. Perhaps many of them."

"Rogue AIs," Maddox said.

"Yes, rogue AIs," Kipling echoed.

"You believe they exist."

"I certainly do."

Maddox gestured toward the door. "Then why did your agent treat me like some nutcase?"

"Because most of the people in this building believe what the general public believes: that rogue AIs and secret AI cults are myths, conspiracy theories touted by the uneducated and uninformed. We're a skeptical lot at the Bureau, and the few investigations we've opened into matters like these over the years never went anywhere. No hard evidence was ever uncovered. Not a shred of proof pointing to brainjacked cults or free-roaming AIs."

"But this…" Maddox began, pointing to the holo display.

"An aberration, mathematically speaking. Unexplainable, perhaps, but not unexpected. Any large enough statistical sample will always have its outliers. That's what most of my colleagues believe these phenomena to be. Anomalies, nothing more." He chuckled. "Some of them call me the Ghost Hunter. And your data, Mr. Maddox, may well turn out to be corroborating evidence, pointing to a ghost I've been hunting for quite some time."

Maddox smoked. The direction things were moving wasn't altogether bad, he told himself. But neither was it going quite the way he'd hoped. On the one hand, he was pleased he hadn't been laughed out of the room by the highfloor FBI man. And he couldn't deny the relief he'd felt when he sensed he'd found an ally in Kipling. But at the same time, the nameless entity wasn't the AI Maddox was worried about at the moment. It wasn't the one ruthlessly hunting him down, dropping hovers out of the sky onto his head.

"Look, I don't mean to sound ungrateful or pushy," Maddox said, knowing he probably sounded both, "but I didn't come here to help with a ghost hunt."

If the datajacker's blunt words bothered Kipling, it didn't show in the man's expression. "No, you didn't."

"Don't get me wrong," Maddox said. "The ghost you're after is nothing but a menace. Something that powerful running around on the loose"—he shook his head—"it's nothing but bad." He recalled how the machine behind the grandmotherly avatar had manipulated him—in its own velvet-gloved way—to do its bidding. How it had brainwashed Lora and thousands of others into thinking it was some cybernetic god that knew the path to enlightenment. How it had even somehow managed to implant a dream into his mind. If he ever had the chance to pull its plug, he'd do so without a moment's hesitation.

"But it's not the one trying to kill you," Kipling said, completing the thought.

Maddox blew smoke. "That's right."

The director stared at Maddox for a ponderous moment. "I'd be lying if I said I believed much of what you've shared with me here this morning. Clandestine AI wars. The Latour-Fisher entity—the most expensive commercial artificial intelligence ever developed—back from the dead without anyone noticing, gone rogue and hell-bent on murder." He narrowed his eyes skeptically. "Extraordinary claims require extraordinary evidence, as the saying goes."

Again, Maddox could hardly fault the man for doubting him. That the FBI man had believed any part of the wild story had been something close to miraculous.

"But I am intrigued, Mr. Maddox, so I'll make you an offer," Kipling said, raising an index finger. "If your information does indeed turn out to be corroborating, I'll look into this Latour-Fisher business."

"Thank you," Maddox said with genuine appreciation. He took a long, deep draw on his cigarette and blew out, finally allowing himself to feel a small amount of relief. He was a long way from out of trouble, but maybe now he was finally heading in that direction. The moment of comfort was short-lived, however, as he thought of the kid, alone and probably worried to death by now.

He rubbed out his cigarette. "There's one other thing," he said. "I need a small favor."

14
NEUROCHEM BOOST

For modern-day mercenaries like Beatrice, mods weren't a luxury, they were a necessity. An indispensable part of the job. Carpenters had hammers. Scientists had microscopes. Datajackers had trodebands and VS decks. Mercs—also known as security specialists—had artificially modified strength, reflexes, and senses.

At a bare minimum, a security specialist needed neurochemical enhancements, the most fundamental of which amplified both the quantity and quality of your body's adrenaline rush. Left unmoderated, a natural surge of adrenaline sharpened your senses, but it also dulled your reasoning. You reacted on instinct, following the lizard brain's binary paths of fight or flight. Neurochem enhancements overrode the lizard brain, amping the advantages of your body's nature while minimizing its inherent flaws. For adrenaline mods, this meant they not only boosted your natural hormonal surge but also suppressed the animal panic that normally came with it, allowing you to think soberly and rationally.

And the latest adrenaline mods, the most expensive ones, the ones only a privileged few like Beatrice could afford, had a new feature: manual control.

Beatrice had kicked off an adrenaline push only once before, a few weeks earlier in the recovery room at her local off-grid clinic. She'd just purchased the mod and wanted to make sure it worked properly. And it had.

Now, ambushed by three people on her charter flight, one of whom was choking her into unconsciousness from behind, it seemed like the right moment for a second press of that particular button. Gasping for air, she bore down the way the medic had told her to, grunting and gritting her teeth until she felt a kind of POP deep inside her brain.

Everything changed instantly. Time slowed to a crawl and she was hyperaware and no longer on the verge of blacking out. Everything around her took on a sudden sharpness. She smelled the cologne of the man holding her down, mingled with the liquor on his breath. She noticed clouds outside the window, felt the chilled air on her cheeks from the overhead vent.

And she was strong, insanely strong. Only a moment before, her arms and legs had been immobilized, but now she shrugged off the man and woman holding her down as if they were small children, sending them tumbling into the seats across the aisle. Then she wriggled two fingers under the cord around her neck, relieving some of the pressure. With an effort, she managed to get her whole hand underneath. The assailant behind her pulled harder, and the cord burrowed into the meat of Beatrice's hand. Temporarily immune to the pain, she pushed against the cord, feeling it slice through her flesh until it dug into bone. She pushed harder, finally making enough room to duck down and free herself. Blood gushing from her wounded hand, she was up and on her feet in the aisle before her attackers could rise from their seats.

Even with a three-to-one advantage, her attackers stood little chance. It was as if they were moving in slow motion. She saw each blow long before it reached her, countering each with her own impossibly fast punches and kicks. Every grab she easily avoided. Every punch she effortlessly dodged. Within seconds it was over. Two of her attackers lay on the jet's cabin floor, beaten into unconsciousness, and the third flailed helplessly in a choke hold.

"Who sent you?" she demanded, tightening her grip around McChatty's neck. "Who are you working for?"

The man sputtered and clawed at her forearm. Blood from her wound soaked her sleeve to the elbow. She felt McChatty's strength ebbing, felt him going limp.

"All right, all right!" McChatty managed to get out. She released him, shoving him to the cabin floor. Kneeling with his forehead pressed against the carpet, he coughed uncontrollably until he caught his breath, then rolled onto his back and lay there gasping.

"Tell me," Beatrice growled. She felt the forced surge of adrenaline begin to wane. That was bad. The biggest downside of adrenaline mods, even the best ones, was the post-surge crash. Biochemists still hadn't worked out how to lessen the fatigue that invariably followed the frantic burst of strength and heightened perception.

The man's breathing finally slowed enough for him to speak. He rose to a sitting position. "You wouldn't believe me if I told—"

She caught sight of the pistol an instant before it fired. She lunged away, the shot missing her as she tumbled into a seat. The copilot (or pilot, Beatrice wasn't sure) stood in the cockpit doorway, smoking pistol in his hand. He had a strangely uncertain look on his face, and he held the gun awkwardly, as if he'd never handled a firearm before. Instead of firing off an immediate second shot, he hesitated, wavering there in the doorway.

Rookie mistake. Beatrice was on top of him in a flash, breaking his wrist and seizing the gun with a single cracking strike. The man howled and doubled over, clutching his injured hand. McChatty tried to surprise her from behind, springing up off the floor and rushing her. Sensing the attack, she spun around and fired, sitting him back down with a single shot to the gut.

Beatrice looked over at her two other attackers. The flight attendant sat with her head back, eyes staring upward and mouth open. The bullet meant for Beatrice had caught her squarely in the forehead. The other woman, the passenger who'd tried to strangle Beatrice, had risen to her feet. Still groggy, she swayed back and forth in the aisle.

"Sit back down," Beatrice barked, training the gun on the woman. Blood oozed from Beatrice's injured hand, dripping from the pistol's handle and staining the beige carpet. She grimaced as a wave of pain struck her.

The man with the broken wrist tackled her from behind, and both tumbled forward to the aisle floor.

The chemically assisted adrenaline was still pumping through her system, and she fought off the man's attempts to wrest the gun from her hand. Her would-be strangler, jolted into alertness by the gunshot, began to kick ferociously at Beatrice's midsection. Not wanting to fire the gun again and risk depressurizing the cabin, Beatrice tried to get to her feet. She was halfway up when the point of the woman's shoe struck her hard in the diaphragm, knocking the wind from her and dropping her to her knees.

Both were on top of her in an instant, punching and kicking and grabbing for the gun. Beatrice couldn't breathe, couldn't get up. Blow after blow landed on her head and midsection as she tried to fend them off. With every passing moment, she could feel the adrenaline boost weaken further. A hard shot struck her just above the ear, and she knew she was moments away from being incapacitated. She rolled onto her back and fired twice. Both her assailants staggered a few steps, then fell to the floor.

Her neck chafed and stinging, her hand in excruciating pain, she slowly rose. One of her attackers, the woman, lay motionless, her eyes staring up at Beatrice in a death stare. The other coughed weakly and attempted to crawl away from her. A moment later he sagged to the floor and stopped moving.

The gun in her uninjured hand, Beatrice turned and peered through the open cockpit door. The pilot sat sideways in his seat, staring wide-eyed at the carnage throughout the cabin. He reached into his jacket.

"Don't do it!" Beatrice shouted, leveling the pistol

at him. "Don't!"

The man didn't comply, removing a small handgun from his jacket. Beatrice fired twice at his midsection before he could raise the weapon. The man dropped the firearm, grimacing painfully, then lurched forward out of his seat and fell to the floor.

Beatrice approached the man and kicked the dropped pistol away, realizing in the next moment the precaution had been unnecessary. The pilot was dead. She lowered the firearm to her side and let out a long breath. She began to feel the steep comedown crash of the neurochem boost, as if someone was siphoning energy from her body. But this was no time to worry about fatigue, she thought, glancing around the jet's interior.

Fifteen thousand feet in the air, with no flying experience whatsoever, Beatrice was the only living soul left on the plane.

15
CURSED

"Tommy's in custody?" Maddox asked, confused.

"Yes," Kipling replied, narrowing his eyes at the holo display. He gestured, increasing the resolution of the local arrest logs. "See here," he said, pointing at one of the entries. "One Thomas Park, verified ID via detailed face and fingerprint scan, blah blah blah." The director ran his eyes down the record. "Looks like they picked him up last night."

"What for?"

"Vagrancy," Kipling said with a chuckle. "That's nice and vague. Resisting arrest too." He poked his head around the floating image and looked directly at Maddox. "Apparently your safe house wasn't all that safe."

Kipling gestured through the police data for another minute, then nodded to himself. "All right, I see what happened. Your safe house is right in the middle of a hot spot D.C. police have been monitoring for drug-fabbing activity. So when your boy shows up in what they think is an abandoned house, they assume he's with the narcos and take him in for questioning."

Maddox sighed. "Wonderful. Now what?" Minutes earlier, Maddox had asked the FBI man if he could bring the kid into protective custody. Kipling had agreed, immediately calling up an app in the table's holo projector and geotagging the safe house address Maddox had given him. As Kipling had tagged the location, a flashing alert had gone off, indicating there'd been a recent arrest at the location.

Now Kipling turned off the alert and waved dismissively. "Nothing to worry about. Give me a minute."

Maddox watched as Kipling made a call in his specs to someone he assumed was someone fairly high up in the D.C. police force.

"Arthur?" Kipling asked. "This is Stellan Kipling over at FBI Data Crimes…Yes, just fine, thanks, and you?…Arthur, I don't want to take much of your time and I hate to be a bother, but I need a small favor related to an investigation I've got going…"

The call lasted less than a minute, and the director's tone never wavered from the sort of casual ease someone else might have while ordering food from a restaurant. When it was over, Kipling said to Maddox, "Charges dropped, your boy should be here within the hour."

Maddox had almost forgotten what could be accomplished with a few words from a highfloor big shot like Kipling. Not since his brief career in the corporate world had Maddox witnessed such an act. He recalled how a higher-up in the company's executive class, the so-called corporati, had only needed a few seconds on a lens call with his China-based counterpart to transform the lives of hundreds of workers in a Kowloon factory, making them jobless victims of company cost-cutting. And a one-minute call from a vice president had sent billions in investment funds to a struggling start-up company, making every one of its fifty employees instantly rich. Power was a kind of magic wand, and those who wielded it—the wealthy or the politically connected—could perform impossible feats with ease.

In less than an hour, Tommy appeared in the meeting room's doorway, accompanied by a security guard. He lifted his chin casually at Maddox.

"What's up, bruh?" the youth said.

Maddox smiled inwardly. The Tommy he'd met two short years ago might have teared up at that moment, overcome by the appearance of a friendly face and the realization he was out of trouble. That kid was apparently gone. This one took it all in stride, cool as you like. Tommy effin' Park.

"Take a seat," Maddox said, and the kid limped forward. "What happened to you?"

"Jumped off a roof," Tommy said, wincing as he sat. "Thought I broke it at first, but it's feeling better now."

Kipling introduced himself to the kid, then turned to Maddox. "I'll leave you two alone to catch up."

When the door closed behind the FBI man, Tommy said, "Who's that?"

"The man who got you out of jail," Maddox said. He started to roll a cigarette.

"I like him already," Tommy said. Then he leaned forward and whispered conspiratorially. "Bruh, is this really FBI HQ?"

"I'm afraid it is, kid."

"And this is the place you came for help?"

Maddox blew smoke. "They're the only operation with the gear and the personnel that could take on an AI. And they're good at protecting people too."

Tommy looked skeptical, so Maddox answered the kid's unvoiced question. "I had an angle with one of their agents."

Tommy nodded slowly. "Okay," he said. "Well, you could have told me all that, you know."

"Maybe I should have," Maddox admitted. He'd left the kid in the safe house, alone and totally out of the loop. "No, I definitely should have," he said a moment later. "It was wrong to keep you in the dark like that."

Tommy waved him off. "Water under the bridge, bruh. You had reasons. I get it." He leaned back in the chair. "So what happens now? They going to help you out or what?"

Maddox drew on his cigarette. "It's one of those 'you help us, we'll help you' kind of things. I have some info this Director Kipling wants. And if it helps him out, he might help get the Latour-Fisher AI off my back."

Tommy nodded appreciatively. "Then I like him even more. So what's our next move?"

"*My* next move, you mean. There's no our in this, kid. Not anymore."

Confusion clouded Tommy's face. "I don't understand."

Maddox swallowed, trying to come up with a way to soften the blow. Searching for words and phrases that might not hurt the kid.

"They're going to put you on a plane," he said, "to Toronto. I want you stay with Beatrice until all this blows over." *If* it all blew over, he added inwardly.

The kid's face dropped. "What? When?"

"Today," Maddox said. "Now, in fact."

The kid winced as if he'd been slapped. "Now? As in now, now?"

"That's right." Maddox nodded toward the door. "They're going to put you in a car and take you to the airport. And you're going to have to go dark too. Stay offline for at least a couple months."

"Have you talked to B about this?"

"Not lately," Maddox admitted, "but when she left us in Manhattan, before everything went sideways, she wanted to take you with her."

"I don't need a babysitter, bruh," the kid snapped.

"I know you don't."

"Then let me stay."

"I can't."

"Why not?"

The datajacker took a long draw on his cigarette and didn't answer. There was nothing but trouble coming Maddox's way. Bad trouble, same as always. He sensed it, felt it in his gut. And while the killer AI had no interest in Tommy—of that he was all but certain—he wanted the kid as far away as possible from whatever madness was coming.

Maddox was the thing's target. And the kid had been standing too close to that target for too long already. He'd be safe with Beatrice. She'd told him as much back in Manhattan, and he should have listened to her before dragging the kid all the way to D.C. It had been foolish of him to think he could protect the kid.

"You need my help," Tommy said, his voice cracking with emotion.

"Not this time, kid."

"So you're just going to shove me out the door?" Tommy said sharply. "Push me away like you pushed B away?"

Maddox blew smoke. "This is my fight, kid. My problem. Not yours."

A hurt look came across the kid's face. "I didn't know there was a difference," he said, his voice dropping with disappointment.

"Tommy, you're leaving," Maddox said, averting his eyes from the kid's pained expression. "End of story."

If the kid stuck around, he'd get hurt, Maddox reminded himself. There was no doubt about that. Because Tommy's mentor was toxic. Cursed. Maddox had never been the superstitious sort, but over these last couple years he'd come to accept there was some kind of black mark on him. He'd come to accept it as a simple truth of his existence, as irrefutable as the color of his eyes and hair. And that black mark was poison. Anyone close to him ended up hurt or dead. The growing list of victims all but proved it. His friend Jack, gone. Rooney, gone. Lora, in her own way, gone. Datajacking rivals and bystanders, crushed by runaway machines and dive-bombing hovers—all dead simply because they'd had the bad luck to cross paths with Blackburn Maddox.

He wasn't going to let Tommy Park get added to that grim list of names.

16
PERSUASIVE ARGUMENT

Maddox had never been good at goodbyes, and the one with Tommy hadn't been an exception to this rule. Moments earlier, when the hurt, angry kid had stood and stormed out of the room, Maddox had wanted to say something. But much in the same way as when Beatrice had walked out on him in Manhattan, words had failed him.

Now he sat alone, staring at the tabletop. His cigarette lay smashed out in the ashtray, a few last wisps of smoke rising from its smoldering tip. He'd done the right thing, he told himself, sending the kid away.

Do you really believe that, boyo?

Kipling entered the room, pausing in the doorway. "Everything go all right? Your young friend didn't seem terribly pleased just now."

"He'll get over it," Maddox said, clearing his throat. "Were you able to reach her?" he asked, referring to Beatrice.

"Not yet," Kipling said. "But we'll keep trying."

The director took a seat. "I'd like to discuss our

next steps."

"Sure," Maddox said, relieved to have his thoughts moved away from the look on Tommy's face.

"I'd like to meet with this ex of yours, Lora, as soon as possible."

Stunned, Maddox didn't say anything for a moment. "I don't know where she is. I told you, all the 'Nettes—"

"Yes, yes," Kipling said, "this rogue AI made all its followers disappear into thin air."

"That's right," Maddox said carefully.

"And yet you had contact with this AI within the last two days." Kipling leaned forward. "Are you saying you *didn't* connect with this rogue entity through your ex? As you explained you had on previous occasions?" The FBI man then adjusted his specs, a not-so-subtle reminder of the bullshit-detecting app he had running on his lenses.

Damn, Maddox thought. Not much got past Kipling. He was a canny one, for sure.

You don't get to the FBI high floors if you aren't sharp, boyo.

To avoid getting caught in a lie, Maddox remained silent. He removed his tobacco bag and began to roll a cigarette.

"I won't arrest her," Kipling said, removing his specs and putting them in his jacket pocket. "You have my word on that. All I want to do is interview her. And her patron as well, if I'm allowed."

Maddox tapped the finished cigarette against the tabletop. He didn't like the direction this was going.

"I thought we had a deal," he said.

"We do," Kipling said. "And if your information proves to be useful, I'll certainly live up to my side of the bargain." Then he added coyly, "Of course, how quickly I can do that is still a bit up in the air, I'm afraid. My department has only so many resources and we're spread quite thin these days."

Maddox frowned, getting the man's point. He reminded himself Stellan Kipling was a cop at the end of the day. A disheveled, mild-mannered cop who occupied a powerful highfloor post, but a cop all the same. And cops never dealt squarely with criminals. Fake plea bargains were dangled like bait to compel confessions. Guarantees of reduced sentences were conveniently forgotten by prosecutors. From the bribe-taking beat cops on the City's floor all the way up to the top of the FBI, cops couldn't be trusted. For a fleeting couple of hours, he'd thought this Kipling might have been made of different stuff. Maybe he wasn't.

"Please," Kipling said earnestly, "I know you think I'm being unfair, but put yourself in my place for a moment. Imagine you've been hunting this…white whale of an AI for years, only catching occasional glimpses of it here and there. Your colleagues chuckle at you, say you're obsessed. But you know you're right and everyone else is wrong. You can feel it, even if you don't have persuasive evidence on your side. Then imagine one day, out of nowhere, corroborating evidence is suddenly within your reach. It's as if your white whale has surfaced right next to your ship, close enough to reach out and touch. You wouldn't just let it disappear again into the depths of the ocean, perhaps never to be seen again, would you?"

Maddox had to hand it to the man. He made a persuasive argument. Persuasive enough that Maddox felt his doubts from only moments before begin to lessen. Not disappear entirely, to be sure, but it was hard to deny the sincerity in the man's face, the authentic plea in his voice.

"Let me put it to you another way," Kipling said. "If I'm able to locate this rogue AI, bring it under control, and free all those people from its grasp, would you see that as a bad thing?"

No, Maddox admitted silently. When he'd lived with Lora, he'd longed for exactly that kind of scenario to play out. He'd wished for some government agency to find the nameless AI and destroy it, severing the tendrils it had burrowed into Lora's mind. The FBI man had made his point: there wasn't much reason for Maddox to try and keep Lora uninvolved. Like her tens of thousands of brain-connected brothers and sisters, she was already involved.

He looked squarely into Kipling's eyes. "You won't arrest her?"

"She was duped," Kipling said. "As they all were. They're victims, not criminals. I can make sure the Bureau treats them as such."

Maddox lit his cigarette, took a long drag. He didn't really know what to make of Kipling. He wanted to believe the man would keep his word, that he'd bring the nameless AI to justice, that he'd help Maddox with his own AI problems, and that he wouldn't put Lora in harm's way. Then he reminded himself Kipling could force Lora's address out of him, but he hadn't. Hadn't yet, anyway. Sitting there across from each other, both men knew Kipling's request was little more than a polite pretense. One way or another, the FBI man could get what he wanted, with as little effort as he'd expended on the phone when he'd sprung Tommy out of jail. And while Maddox was a long way from trusting the man completely, he appreciated Kipling's effort to maintain the charade, to pretend Maddox actually had a choice in the matter. There was something to be said for someone who made room for a small bit of civility in an uncivilized world.

"Fine," the datajacker said, blowing smoke. "I can take you there."

17
HOW DO YOU LAND A JET?

Hired fist. Mercenary. Security consultant. Whatever name you cared to put on what Beatrice did for a living, she'd been in the business for most of her adult life. She'd worked with heads of state, CEOs, narco kingpins, movie stars, sports celebrities. Her gigs spanned a wide variety of security needs, from straightforward bodyguard work or simple surveillance to complex protection service for entire government departments, managing dozens of security personnel. Most of her jobs had been on the legal side of things, but she'd discreetly worked the other side from time to time, when the pay had justified the risk. And like Maddox, she'd once had a mentor who'd trained her well, who'd taught her everything he'd known about surveillance, marksmanship, combat tactics, and protective security, preparing her to take on any situation.

Well, *almost* any situation.

Beatrice glanced around the jet's cabin, fighting down a surge of panic. She had to breathe, had to think. The plane—on autopilot she assumed—flew along steadily for the moment. Her injured hand throbbed painfully, blood still flowing freely from the nasty gash.

First things first, she thought. She had to bind her wound. Searching the cabin, she spotted a long scarf around the neck of the seated woman, the one who'd been hit by the stray bullet. Stepping over bodies, she removed the seated woman's neckwear. As she began to wrap it around her hand, she noticed something strange about the exit wound behind the woman's ear. There was something there, something that didn't look like gore or blood. Leaning in for a better look, Beatrice gasped in recognition. Covered in blood, the tech that had been in the woman's head moments before hung grotesquely by a thin strand of flesh.

Brainjacks! The woman had brainjacks.

Beatrice knelt down to the body nearest her, the one she'd dubbed McChatty. Running her finger behind his ear, she felt a small indentation. She brushed away the man's hair and subvocalized a command, increasing the color sensitivity of her implanted eyes. She spied a slightly discolored patch and worked her finger underneath what she knew it to be, a brainjack cover-up. Peeling it away revealed three rectangular slots the width of a fingernail.

"Jesus," she muttered, then darted from body to body, checking each one and finding the same thing. Everyone on the plane—everyone except her—had brainjacks. They were all 'Nettes. Even the pilot and copilot. They were a goddamned 'Nette hit squad.

For a long moment, Beatrice stared at the bodies in stunned disbelief, at the holes drilled into their skulls. Why would 'Nettes want her dead? And how had they managed to take over this charter? For that matter, how'd they known she'd taken it in the first place? She thought back to the last-minute cancellation of her commercial flight and to the seemingly fortunate availability of a charter, conveniently headed in her direction just when she'd needed it. Had it not been for the attempt on her life, she might have seen it as nothing more than one unlucky break followed by a lucky one. But Beatrice had seen the kind of manipulations an AI could perform, how it could surreptitiously lead someone down a path like a lab mouse prompted through a maze.

The jet hit a patch of turbulence, and the aircraft's shudder jarred her back to the present. The plane, she thought desperately. There was no one flying the plane.

She moved to the cockpit, dragged the pilot from his seat, and dumped him on the cabin floor. Sitting down, she ran her eyes across the control panel, a continuous screen running the width of the cockpit, subdivided into smaller displays. A graphic of the jet occupied the center, the image surrounded by feeds and digitized dial readouts. Altimeter, airspeed, vertical speed, heading, radar, throttle, fuel, GPS. She was relieved to find a flashing indicator that told her the autonav was engaged. The two W-shaped control wheels gently tilted and twisted in small synchronized movements, under automated control.

Everything looked okay, as far as she could tell. The plane was flying straight, neither gaining nor losing altitude. And it wasn't crashing, which was good. Could the thing land itself?

Passenger airline pilots, unlike so many other occupations, hadn't been supplanted by AIs or intelligent systems. While fully automated flight had been technologically possible for generations and used extensively by the military and the cargo-shipping industry, the public had never become comfortable with pilot-less passenger flights. Ground cars and hovers, yes, but an airplane with no human at the controls had been a technological leap of faith the vast majority of travelers were still reluctant to make. But did that mean the onboard systems *couldn't* land a plane? Or did it mean that they simply didn't? Beatrice had no idea.

In her implants, she blinked up a search window, nearly laughing at the absurdity of the text that appeared from her subvocalized thought: *How do you land a jet?*

Five minutes and several searches later, she'd found answers to most of her questions. Yes, the autonav could land the plane quite easily. If the system wasn't toggled off, it would automatically follow the flight plan, communicate with the tower, and land on the designated runway. It was a safety feature built into all passenger jet control systems, a redundancy to ensure a safe landing in case the flight crew lost consciousness from a sudden loss of pressure at high altitude. Or if they were killed in a botched hit job, she added inwardly.

So she wouldn't die in a plane crash. Under any other circumstances, the revelation would have resulted in tremendous relief. But as she turned and glanced back at the carnage in the main cabin, she frowned, knowing her problems were far from over. Soon she'd have to exit the plane, probably with airport rescue and security teams waiting outside the door, alerted by the autonav's emergency beacon.

Maybe there'd be police too. But whoever ended up greeting her as she stepped down the ladder, it was a safe bet she wouldn't be able to just smile and walk past them with her bag over her shoulder and go find a taxi. Not with five bodies lying in the cabin.

She sighed. So she was going to have to do this the hard way. Wonderful. She blinked up the search window again, and for the second time she subvocalized her original query: *How do you land a jet…*

Only this time, she added the words *without autonav?*

18
OVERPRICED SPECS

"Bruh, I'm starving," Tommy said again, fidgeting in his chair.

"You just ate on the plane," the suit to his left said.

"But that was, what, a whole half hour ago?" Tommy said. "And it was a baby portion besides." His FBI babysitters, the two suits seated on either side of him, exchanged a tired look. At last, he thought. He'd been working on them since D.C., and now he was finally starting to get under their skin.

Tommy sat between the suits in a mostly empty waiting lounge at LaGuardia—just as he'd sat between them on the shuttle flight from D.C.— waiting for his connection to Toronto. He wondered if someone had finally reached Bea, if she'd gotten word yet that he was on his way. Not that he had any intention of boarding the flight that would take him to her, of course.

"Seriously," Tommy whined, "I'm starting to feel kinda lightheaded. I think I'm, like, diabetic or some shit."

The suit to his right, the older one, looked up at

the display with flight arrival and departure details. "They're boarding in fifteen minutes," he said gruffly. "Get something on the plane."

Tommy held out his hand, palm down and fingers spread. "Look, bruh, I'm totally shaking," he said. "I gotta eat something now or I might pass out, I'm telling you."

The younger suit, the more annoyed one, caved, letting out a long breath. "All right, all right," he snapped, "what do you want?" He stood up.

Tommy tilted his head toward the door leading to the terminal. "Noodle stand out there to the right. Any spicy noodles are fine. I'm not picky, bruh." The man started to leave, then jerked to a stop when Tommy blurted out, "And apple soda if they have it." The suit frowned and turned away. "And don't forget the peanut sauce," Tommy hollered to the man's back as the agent exited the lounge. "Peanut sauce, bruh!"

He let a minute pass before he stood up and headed toward the lounge restroom. "Sit down," the older suit said. "You can go on the plane."

Tommy shifted his weight from one foot to the other and put a worried look on his face. "Not really sure I can wait."

"Jesus," the suit said, muttering something else under his breath as he rose. "Make it quick."

Tommy headed to the restroom, unsure of his next move. He hadn't really planned anything out, aside from separating the two suits. If he had to make a run for it, he had a better chance of ditching one of them than two. He passed through the restroom entrance, glancing furtively behind him as he turned the corner. The suit didn't follow him in, stationing himself just outside the entry, which was the only way in or out. Inside, Tommy relieved himself at a urinal, glancing around the white-tiled space. As he washed up, a door at the end of the toilet row opened and a janitor emerged, pushing a rolling bucket with a mop handle sticking up out of it. He locked the door behind him with a key card attached to his belt loop by a string. Tommy looked around. There was no one else around.

Leaning over the basin, he dried his hands slowly, waiting for the janitor to pass behind him, then he whirled around and bumped hard into the man.

"What the hell, young fella?" the man said, knocked backwards a step.

"Oh, sorry, mister," Tommy said. "Didn't see you there. My bad."

The man gave him a sour look and continued on his way, pushing his bucket before him and disappearing out into the lounge. Tommy moved toward the door the janitor had exited a moment earlier, the stolen key card in his hand. He unlocked the door with the card and stepped into a closet-sized storeroom filled with cleaning products. Despite the harsh chemical smell, Tommy grinned, spying a second door and unlocking it. He stepped through into a narrow passageway that ran parallel to the terminal. He ran down the empty corridor, putting as much distance between him and the lounge as possible, until he came to a door with a sign over it reading TERMINAL B ENTRANCE. Breathing hard and expecting a facility-wide alarm to go off at any moment, he pushed through the door and stepped out into a noisy, crowded terminal. He slipped into the flowing current of people, putting more distance between him and the lounge as he searched for the nearest exit. Nakedfaced among the almost totally bespectacled crowd, he felt conspicuous as hell. Then he saw it above a large archway—the most beautiful four-letter word imaginable, bright red and beckoning him: EXIT.

He turned toward the archway, then did a double take as someone caught his eye. Tommy gasped, instantly recognizing the profile as the person turned his head.

Blackburn fucking Maddox walked three meters in front of him, flanked by two of the FBI fooks Tommy had seen in D.C. What were the odds? Only hours ago, he'd thought he'd seen his mentor for maybe the last time, and now here he was, almost close enough to kick in the rear. And no small part of Tommy wanted to do exactly that: give the man a nice swift ass-kick for tossing him aside, for making him feel like he was unwanted baggage. But screw him, he thought, pushing down a surge of resentment and rejection. If he wanted to fly solo, let him do it. He headed to the exit and left the terminal, barely managing to hold back tears.

* * *

Just beyond airport property, there was a sprawling marketplace Tommy had seen a few times on feeds but had never visited until now. A jumbled chaos of hundreds of food kiosks, tiny cafes, and shop stalls, it catered to budget travelers who didn't want to pay exorbitant airport prices. Tommy's ground cab slowly navigated the improvised roadway that twisted and turned through the bazaar's dense confusion of vendors, shoppers, and street barkers.

"Stop here for a second," Tommy told the driver, spotting a spec stand. He stepped out of the car before it had come to a complete stop, knowing he had to hurry. By now the suits were looking for him, and maybe cops too. He couldn't hang around for long.

"Got any veils?" he asked the stand's proprietor, a kid who looked about his own age.

The kid shook his head. "Those are illegal," he said, then waved his hand across the specs lined up across the counter. "All's I got is what you see here."

Tommy straightened up, gave the kid a bullshit-cutting look. "Bruh, come on." He placed a stack of cash on the counter.

The kid looked left and right, then discreetly swept the bills off the counter and pocketed them. From somewhere underneath, he removed a pair of specs and placed them on the countertop. "Stack of five," he said, meaning the specs came preloaded with five stolen IDs.

Tommy frowned, knowing he'd just been ripped off. The wad of cash should have gotten him a ten-stack at least, but he didn't have time to argue or haggle for a better deal. "Thanks," he grunted and put the lenses, a pair of knockoff Venturellis, on his face as he returned to the waiting cab and climbed in.

A mile outside the airport, Tommy's thudding heart finally began to slow down. He leaned back in the cab's seat and let out a long breath. You didn't get a freebie flight to Toronto every day, he reflected, feeling a bit as if he'd missed out on an opportunity. But he'd made his own way since he was twelve, deciding where he'd go and when and how. He wasn't going to be forced to go anywhere, by anyone. And besides that, if he stayed with Bea the feds might keep tabs on him. And he couldn't very well get back to datajacking for a living if he was standing in a federal spotlight, could he?

On his new specs, a flashing message on the lens told him the device was still in standby mode. As the car merged onto the BQE and headed toward Manhattan, Tommy stepped through the specs' setup routine, adjusting the device to his preferred eye movements and frame taps. As cheap knockoffs, they had no brain wave sensors in the temple arms, so he didn't have to bother calibrating subvocalizations. When he finished the setup, he popped in the first ID, a Manhattan-based subway worker. Then he fanned through the preloaded apps, disappointed to find a paltry selection of crapware. The half dozen outdated apps only reminded him how much he'd overpaid. He glanced over the settings of the final app, an encryption package. He was pleased to find he recognized it, having used the very same version a few times over the last year. It was a copy of a recent military package, modded by Crackhead Bob, a street techie out of the Bronx, well known in datajacking circles. Bob's crypto app was a solid build.

As the taxi moved through heavy traffic, he debated the wisdom of calling Beatrice. Going online right now in any way was risky—even just for a one-minute call with watertight crypto. That killer AI might have bots out there everywhere looking for his data profile and listening for his voice signature. And even if it didn't, by now the feds might have had their own pet AIs sniffing around for him.

But he had to let her know he was all right. And he had to let her know what had gone down, because this whole mess involved her too.

He kicked off the crypto app, changed his caller

ID from the default to a name she'd recognize, then from memory called Beatrice's private number. A few moments later she answered.

"Hey, mama," he said, "what's happening?" He listened to her reply, which ended in a question. Her voice sounded unusually stressed.

"No," he answered, confused, "I don't know how to fly a jet. Why are you asking?"

19
CHANGE OF HANDS

The hover approached Manhattan from the east, a sky of gray clouds brushing the uppermost floors of the tallest hiverises and standalone buildings. Maddox recognized the familiar profile of East Harlem as it emerged from the mist. His home turf, as recognizable as his own reflection in the hover's paned glass. Harlem had street art unlike anywhere else, and its residents took tremendous pride in the originality and pervasiveness of their local creations. In most of the City, graffiti usually reached a height of around twenty stories, sometimes a bit higher or lower, depending on the wealth of the building's residents. If your floor's facade was free of street art, it denoted a certain level of prestige and privilege, so the more affluent residents—usually around the twentieth floor or so—often pooled money and contracted monthly sandblasting services to keep their floor's outer shell in its pristine, unblemished state. In the City, appearances mattered.

But in Harlem, and in particular East Harlem, Maddox's old stomping grounds, street art was a source of community pride and identity. Buildings were often tattooed from head to toe, and proudly so. It wasn't uncommon for a complex mural, years in the making, to cover the entire side of a hundred-story hiverise. East Harlem was the City's bustling burst of color.

Watching the eastern edge of Manhattan grow larger, Maddox sat in the passenger seat as Nguyen directed the hover's autonav to take the nearest southbound transit lane. Half an hour earlier, Maddox, Nguyen, and Kipling had landed at LaGuardia in one of the Bureau's jets. Kipling had parted company with them at the airport, heading to a meeting at the local field office, after which he'd meet the datajacker and Agent Nguyen at a cafe on the same block as Lora's condo building. And assuming she was home, Kipling's idea was to interview her. Whether or not she'd consent to an interview—much less put him in contact with her beloved AI—was another matter, of course.

"So what did you tell him?" Nguyen said, referring to Maddox's chat with his superior. The agent's disposition toward Maddox, though it had never been warm in the first place, had grown colder, even hostile, since Maddox's extended private meeting with his superior. Maddox sensed Nguyen had been waiting anxiously for the moment he could get the datajacker alone and grill him about it.

"Nothing that'll tarnish your rep," Maddox said, "if that's what you're getting at."

Nguyen didn't appear to believe that. "You don't have anything to worry about," Maddox assured him.

"All that business about selling me out yesterday morning," Nguyen said. "It was a bluff, wasn't it?"

"It was the only play I had," Maddox said. Then, without a hint of regret in his voice, he added, "Sorry."

The agent gave him a sharp look. "Well, now you've got a better play, don't you? All this nonsense about rogue AIs and secret cults. How did you know that would be music to Kipling's ears? How did you know you'd be able to jerk him around like this?"

"I'm not jerking him around," Maddox said. "And I didn't even know his name before today."

"Sure you didn't," Nguyen said.

They didn't speak for the rest of the ride. Nguyen occupied himself with some task in his specs, and Maddox, nakedfaced, watched the ever-bustling coming and going of the transit lanes, stacked above and below their own slowly moving level. As they passed over the green expanse of Central Park, he wondered how things would progress from here. He'd started the snowball on its downhill roll by walking into Nguyen's office yesterday, and now it had gained speed and momentum and had grown to an unstoppable size. He hadn't expected everything to move so fast, but here he was. Actually, thinking back on it, he hadn't really known what to expect at all. His decision to show up at FBI headquarters had been one of desperation, the panicked lunge of an animal trapped in a corner. The screaming sprint of a man with his clothes on fire. Despite the positive development with Kipling, a large part of him still felt the impulsive move had been a big mistake.

Spilled milk, boyo. No use torturing yourself over it.

Maybe so, Roon. Maybe so.

The hover approached Central Park West, beginning its slow descent into the lower, more congested lanes. A couple minutes later, the vehicle's autonav ceded control to the docking system of a parking garage near Lora's building. Darkness fell over the hover as it slid sideways out of the daylight and into the multistoried facility, floating down the row and finally settling into an empty nook with the telltale hiss-clank of the locking mechanism.

"Kipling ought to be here in about forty minutes," Nguyen said, opening his door. "How about you buy me a cup of coffee? It's the least you can do after all the hell you're putting me through."

"My pleasure," Maddox said, matching snark for snark. He opened his own door, stepped out onto the walkway, and headed toward the elevator. The garage was nearly full of parked hovers on this level, but empty of people other than Maddox and Nguyen. As they headed toward the elevator, the agent fell in behind Maddox. Reaching the elevator doors, Maddox began to reach for the sensor to call a car.

"Don't bother," Nguyen said. Turning, Maddox saw the agent holding a gun on him.

"What are you doing?" Maddox asked reflexively.

"What should have been done a long time ago," Nguyen said cryptically.

"You're not doing anything," a voice called.

Two large men, clad in matching oversized specs and black trench coats, jogged up from seemingly nowhere. Each gripped a pistol, and both were trained on Nguyen.

"Put it down," the second man said.

His weapon still pointed at Maddox, Nguyen gave the two new arrivals a fiery look. "What do you think you're doing?" he demanded.

"We're taking the jacker with us," the first man

said. "Drop the weapon, now."

For a long moment, no one spoke. Pistols remained in their threatening positions, one on Maddox and two on Nguyen. Finally, Nguyen lowered his gun, then returned it to the holster under his jacket. "Big mistake you're making," he chided the men. "Huge." His tone, Maddox noticed, had the ring of familiarity. Nguyen knew these men.

The first man called the elevator while the second one covered Nguyen. When the car arrived, the man grasped Maddox by the upper arm and hustled him into the lift. The first man followed, and the doors slowly closed over the image of Nguyen standing with his hands on his hips, his eyes locked on Maddox in a furious stare.

As the car descended, Maddox asked his new minders, "Who are you?"

The two men gave each other a knowing look. Then Maddox felt something hard poke his ribs. Looking down, his eyes widened at the small shockstick, its hot end pressing against him.

"We're your saviors," the first man replied as he flicked the device's switch. A painful jolt surged through Maddox's body, and then everything went black.

20
ONE EIGHTY

"I thought you were in D.C.," Beatrice said. "What happened?"

"I was," Tommy explained. "Then they brought me back to New York. Actually, they were going to put me on a plane to Toronto, but I said screw that. I mean, nothing against your turf, you know, I just wasn't going to play their game. I mean, I don't know Toronto from nothing, so why would I—"

"Tommy, listen to me," Beatrice interrupted.

Moments earlier, when she'd felt the vibration of an incoming call on her pocketed specs, she'd had no intention of answering. Trapped in a jet that would soon land itself with five dead bodies in the cabin, she couldn't imagine any call that might be worth taking at the moment. Then the caller ID had popped up in the corner of her vision, displayed by the feed into her ocular implants: SEYMOUR BUTTS. Recognizing the caller ID as one of Tommy's preferred aliases, she'd answered.

She quickly explained her dire situation to the kid, though she didn't mention her attackers were 'Nettes.

Revealing that, she knew, would set the kid off into question-asking mode, and at the moment she didn't have time for a lengthy Q&A session. And it wasn't like she had any answers, anyway. The kid stayed quiet as she recounted what had happened, except for a few muttered *oh shits*.

"Why would anyone want to take you out?" Tommy asked.

"No idea," she replied. "But I've got other things on my mind right now, kiddo." A flashing message on the cockpit dashboard screen told her the plane would land in twenty-eight minutes.

"Oh, yeah, right," the kid said. "The plane. You need to turn it around and come back here so we can figure a way out of this mess."

"Sure, I'll get right on that," Beatrice said. "Oh, wait, I forgot something. I'm not a trained pilot."

"Hang on a second," Tommy said, then his voice changed in tone, as he began to speak to someone else. "Hey, driver, can you pull over to that noodle stand right there? No, not that one, the one with the yellow sign."

Beatrice felt a surge of frustration. "Seriously, kid?"

"Take it easy, mama," he said. "Guy's gotta eat, right? Listen, give me a minute or two to look through some wares."

"What are you talking about?"

"You know those underground apps that can override nav systems on ground cars and hovers? I figure there's gotta be one out there for jets, right?"

The kid seemed casually optimistic, a sentiment Beatrice didn't share. Wares that hacked into cars' and hovers' operating systems had been around for ages;

joyriding kids used them all the time. Every private vehicle owner was familiar with the routine patch updates and system upgrades designed to plug whatever new hole had been discovered. But private jets? Beatrice had never heard of an app that hacked into an airplane's OS.

But then again, it wasn't like she had a lot of options.

"All right, go take a look," she said, "and hurry."

"On it, B," the kid said.

Another flashing message appeared on the screen. INCOMING COMMS, PLEASE RESPOND. At her feet, two headsets with bulky ear coverings lay on the cabin floor. She picked up one and pressed the padded cup against her ear. "This is flight control at Reagan International, do you copy? Repeat, we've received a distress beacon from your aircraft's automated—"

Beatrice dropped the headphones back to the floor. Outside, a crystal-blue sky stretched to every horizon, painted with wisps of clouds that looked like a painter's casual brushstrokes. A beautiful vista under any other circumstances.

"I think I found something," Tommy chirped in her ear. In the next moment, an app download request flashed on her specs. She blinked yes and subvocalized a command to run the app when the download finished.

"All right, let me try to walk you through it," Tommy said, then she heard an unmistakable slurping sound.

"Maybe you'd like to call me back when you finish your meal?" she said.

"Oh, sorry." Beatrice pictured him wiping his

mouth with his sleeve.

At his request, she gave the kid control of the app in her specs, and he cycled through a series of menus. It was slow going, fraught with missteps, wrong turns, and the kid's muttered curses. He'd never used the app before, so he was learning as he went. Beatrice sat there, barely able to follow what he was doing. He'd call up a menu, drill down to a certain point, then enter a few lines of what she supposed was source code, apparently making changes to the app. As a hired fist, she had little in the way of technical sophistication outside of the surveillance and security wares used by those in her professional field. So like it or not, she was in the kid's hands.

Minutes passed. Beatrice grew more anxious as the cockpit display counted down the jet's arrival time. Fifteen minutes until the wheels touched down on a D.C. runway. Sixteen minutes, she thought darkly, until she was in handcuffs and arrested for a multiple homicide.

"Okay, I'm in," the kid said. Beatrice supposed he meant he'd breached the jet's OS. "Here's what I'm gonna do," he said, then after a short pause added, "or try to do, I mean."

The app, he explained, didn't technically take over the autonav system. As one of the jet's most critical safety features, the autonav subsystem was apparently all but jacker-proof. Instead, the app fooled the autonav by altering the flight plan of record, which according to the kid was archived in a more easily breached portion of the jet's OS. Half of what he said was techie gibberish, but she got the general drift. Tommy would update the flight plan with a revised destination geotag, and the autonav would steer the plane to the updated location—and land it safely, which was quite important to Beatrice.

Also, the kid added, the location didn't have to be an airport. As long as the new destination had a viable landing site, the autonav would set the plane down pretty much anywhere. In a field, on a deserted highway, on a homemade dirt runway.

This last caught Beatrice's attention. "Are you sure about that?"

"That's what the app's telling me," the kid replied. "Just tell me where you want to touch down and we'll try it out."

"Give me a second." She pulled up a map in her specs, pinpointing a landing spot and passing the geotag to Tommy.

"Uh, are you sure about that?" the kid asked.

"Do it," she said. She glanced at the clock. "And hurry up. If it doesn't work, I'll have to come up with a plan B pretty quick."

Ten seconds later the kid said, "All right, done."

Beatrice held her breath and waited. Nothing happened. The jet continued on its unchanged course. "Try again," she said.

"Give it a second," the kid said. "Everything looks good from my end."

"Kid," she said curtly, "from my end nothing happened. I'm still flying in the same—"

The jet abruptly banked, nearly toppling Beatrice out of her seat. She looked down at the instrument screen, searching until she found the directional thingamajig. Slowly, the compass-like instrument rotated, then stopped as the plane leveled out once more, completing a one-eighty-degree turn.

"It worked," she muttered in disbelief. "Jesus,

Mary, and Joseph, I think you did it."

"No shit?" the kid said, sounding as surprised as she was. "I mean, yeah, of course it worked."

"All right, then," she said, letting out a long breath. "I want you to meet me there, okay? And keep a low profile, Tommy. Ultra-low. No plugging in, no online spec connections. Not even calls, understand?"

For a moment he didn't say anything, and she thought the call might have dropped…or been cut. But then she heard the slurping sound again, and the kid replied, barely intelligible through a mouthful of noodles, "Sure, mama. See you there."

21
THE PILE REVISITED

Tommy hadn't been to Jersey in a while, and he liked it that way. Though he was born and raised only a few miles away in the Bronx neighborhood of Hunt's Point, Jersey always seemed like some distant other world. A vast expanse of overgrown lots thick with weeds, crumbling homes long since abandoned, and ghost town industrial complexes, Tommy never thought of New Jersey as a part of the City, though of course it was. For him the City was the clustered hiverises of Manhattan, the teeming crowds of the streets, the neon glow of its towering holo ads. Like his mentor—or his former mentor, he thought sourly—he never felt comfortable outside the five boroughs that made up the City's inner core, its soul.

He sat on his motorbike, its engine idling, on a long flat pan of concrete. A deserted industrial complex stretched out around him. Enormous cranes in the near distance that had once loaded and unloaded ships docked on the Hudson River stood motionless like enormous giants of rusted steel. Crumbling buildings and warehouses dotted the landscape around him, and about a hundred meters away stood the Pile. That was what Beatrice had called it a couple years ago, the last and only other time he'd been here. Originally a shantytown of sorts, founded by a tribe of squatters who'd since migrated elsewhere, the Pile was a cobbled-together mass of old cargo containers, thousands of them, roofed with a patchwork of corrugated aluminum and cheap fiberboard. Inside, miles of tunnels ran through the structure like arteries, and it was through the Pile's twisting, turning innards that he and Beatrice had outmaneuvered a police chase. The Pile sat on a vast, mostly empty expanse of cracked, sunbaked concrete. An ideal spot for a plane to make an automated landing.

He scanned the western horizon for any sign of Beatrice's ride. She wouldn't be coming from the east, he knew. Manhattan airspace was restricted to hover traffic only, and surely the autonav would fly around it. He'd arrived fifteen minutes earlier, and already he'd grown impatient with waiting. Blinking up her number, he started to call her to check in but then stopped. She'd told him to stay offline. Not even calls, she'd insisted.

A smudge in the overcast distance appeared, flying at low altitude, white lights blinking. That had to be her, he thought, growing more certain with every passing moment as the smudge grew larger, taking on the unmistakably sleek profile of a private jet. Half a minute later, watching the jet land was a strange kind of agony. He knew Beatrice was in there, probably sweating bullets, helplessly reliant on some street-modded tech neither of them had ever used or even heard of before today. As the jet made its final approach, he tried not to picture it crashing, its landing gear hitting some crater in the concrete, sending the plane cartwheeling out of control and bursting into flames. Holding his breath, he watched, his neck, shoulders, and face tight with tension, as the aircraft touched down and white puffs of smoke came from the tires.

He let his breath out again as the plane began to slow, eventually stopping a short distance away. Relieved beyond words, he revved his motor and popped the clutch, crouching over the bike's gas tank as it lurched forward. The aircraft's side door yawned open just as he braked to a stop alongside. Beatrice quickly descended the steps and rushed over to him.

"Welcome to Jersey, B," he said. She grabbed his head between her hands and kissed him hard on the mouth, taking him completely by surprise.

"You little shit," she said, mussing the kid's hair, "you saved my ass."

Tommy blushed and tried to play it cool. "No problem, mama," he said, his voice cracking.

Beatrice hopped on the back of his bike. "Let's get out of here, fast," she said. "Air traffic controllers were hollering nonstop over the comms in the last few minutes. We're lucky police hovers aren't here already."

"Probably will be pretty quick," Tommy said. "Hang on."

He gunned the engine and raced across the flat stretch of concrete, winding up through the gears in quick succession. Had it not been for the noise of his motor, the pair would have heard ambulance and fire engine sirens in the distance, growing louder. A minute later, the first police hover arrived on the scene, touching down near the abandoned jet. But by then Tommy and Beatrice were long gone.

*　　*　　*

They headed north, moving more or less parallel to the Hudson River, winding their way through a vast ghost town of crumbling residentials. Tommy knew there were squatters scattered about here and there, holed up in the few ancient dwellings that still had some semblance of a structure, but he knew he wouldn't see any of them. They were shut-ins, mostly. Hermit types.

He'd chosen this particular getaway route for more than its depopulated emptiness, though. The eastern edge of Jersey also had very good cover. Vast canopies of trees, their wild growth unchecked by human pruning for over a century, had grown together, forming a nearly constant roof of verdant green leaves above most of the area's roadways. Tommy and Beatrice were all but hidden from any airborne drones or hovers. Not that there were any, he noted with satisfaction. In the few open spots they'd passed through, he'd checked overhead and seen nothing. Once he'd been certain their getaway had been a clear one, he'd dropped down into second gear, moving along at a safer, more measured clip.

"Stop up here for a minute," Beatrice said in his ear, gesturing toward a cement overpass arching above the road. When they entered the overpass's shadow, Tommy braked the bike to a stop, and Beatrice slid off the back of the seat.

"So what the hell's going on, B?" She'd given him the short version on their call earlier, and since then he'd been dying to find out more.

"Somebody wants me dead," she said, moving

125

around to the front of the bike, "but I don't know why."

"Somebody?" Tommy asked. "You don't know who?"

Even in the shadow of the overpass, Tommy noted an unmistakable darkening of Beatrice's expression. "It's more of a something than a someone."

As it dawned on Tommy what she was talking about, his mouth dropped open. "No way. That AI's after you too?"

"Not the Latour-Fisher AI," Beatrice corrected. "The other one."

Confused, Tommy said, "The old beach lady AI Maddox talked to? The one connected to all those 'Nettes?"

"That's right." She told him about the brainjacks she'd discovered on her attackers.

"Jesus," Tommy gasped. Then he shook his head. "But why?"

"That's what I'd like to know," Beatrice said. She told him she couldn't come up with any reasonable explanation behind it. If the Latour-Fisher entity had returned from the dead and was on the loose as the kid had told her, she could see why *that* AI might want to take her out. Assuming the thing had vengeful tendencies, of course. But the other AI, the nameless one, what reason could *it* possibly have to put out a hit on her? Sure, maybe she wasn't exactly the thing's friend, and unlike Maddox she'd never spoken with it. But for a time hers and the AI's interests had been aligned. They'd shared a common enemy and fought together against it. The fact that Beatrice and the nameless AI had once been allies made it hard to imagine—especially after over two years with no contact whatsoever—that suddenly they'd become enemies. Still, there was no denying she'd been attacked by the thing's followers. There were five corpses back in that jet, and every one of them had brainjacks.

"I've been turning it over for hours, and I still have no idea," Beatrice confessed.

Tommy nodded. "All right, then. Hop on and let's go find some answers."

"What are you talking about?"

"Maddox's ex," the kid said. "She's a 'Nette, remember?"

"You know where she is?"

The kid smiled. "That I do, mama."

A moment of amazement, then an approving grin slowly stretched across Beatrice's face. In the two years she'd known Tommy Park, there were two things about him that never failed to impress her: his insatiable appetite for Thai noodles, and the way he always managed to find a bit of daylight when things seemed their darkest. She climbed onto the seat behind him. "All right, let's get moving."

22
NEW HARDWARE

Consciousness came to Maddox slowly, as bits and pieces of reality aroused his senses. Sounds came first. In the blackness behind his eyelids he became aware of a steady beeping. Faint at first, it gradually grew louder, until some awakening part of him realized it was a nearby device of some sort. He was also aware of a person—no, there were two people—quietly shuffling around him. A man and a woman, murmuring to one another, but Maddox couldn't make out what they were saying. Like smelling salts to a punch-drunk boxer, the woman's flowery perfume helped waken him further. With a great effort, he opened his eyes and forced himself awake. Blinding light hit him like a slap. He gasped and reflexively squeezed his eyes shut again.

"He's starting to come around," the woman's voice said.

"Looks like it," the man answered. Maddox recognized neither voice.

"You should go tell them," the woman said.

"All right," the man said, followed by the sound of

a door opening and closing.

The datajacker opened his eyes again. His blurred vision began to find focus, and the room around him took shape. He was lying on a bed, he realized. A red-haired woman wearing a disposable medical mask over her nose and mouth leaned over him.

"Can you hear me?" she asked.

He tried to answer, but instead of words an incoherent garble came out of his mouth. His head was killing him, and he felt sick to his stomach.

"Try to relax," the woman said.

Feeling nauseous, he closed his eyes again and tried to steady himself. He breathed in through his nose, struggling to remember what had happened, how he'd come to wherever this place was.

He'd been hit with a shockstick! That was it. He felt a bruise-like soreness on his ribs, the spot where he'd been tagged. Yes, he'd been shocked and knocked out. Now he remembered. But by who? The cops? No, that wasn't it. He'd been *with* a cop at the time, hadn't he? Yes, he had.

The fog over his mind began to dissipate, and within a few moments pieces of memory began to drop into place, forming a coherent chain of events. He and Agent Nguyen had been on the way to Lora's place. Then Nguyen had pulled a gun on Maddox in a parking garage, apparently intent on killing him, when two men had appeared, interrupting the execution. The unknown pair had taken custody of the datajacker and then tagged him with a shockstick.

He opened his eyes again and looked around, fighting against a surge of vertigo. The woman had her back to him, finger-swiping her way through a holo display's feed. She wore blue medical scrubs.

They were in a small room, and next to his bed an array of devices beeped and projected small holo displays. Biometric readouts, he realized. Pulse rate, blood oxygen, brain waves, breaths per minute. Had his attackers taken him to a hospital? He'd been knocked out, sure, but had he been so badly injured that he'd needed medical care?

Now more or less awake, he was aware of an oxygen line uncomfortably inserted into his nose. He reached up to remove it, but his arm didn't work. No, that wasn't it. Both his arms worked, but they were being held down by something. He looked down at his body, finding his wrists and ankles restrained. What the hell was this?

Hearing him stir, the woman began to turn around. Maddox quickly shut his eyes again. A moment later the woman said, "Can you hear me?" Then he felt a light tapping on his forehead. "Hey there," the woman said, "anybody home?"

Maddox didn't react, faking unconsciousness. He heard the squeak of a door opening.

"Sorry," the woman said to whoever had entered. "I thought he was coming around. Looks like it's going to be a while longer." The door closed again.

Eyes shut and listening carefully, Maddox waited for the woman to leave the room before daring to open his eyes again. When she finally left him alone minutes later, he took a good look around. If this place was a hospital, it was the nicest, most modern one Maddox had ever seen. Not that he was an expert, of course, but the small room had what appeared to be very expensive state-of-the-art equipment. Even the bed he was strapped into was a technological marvel. It coddled him, molding its shape to the contours of his body, and it had some kind of cooling mechanism that kept his underside comfortable and dry. Even in his current state, it felt better than the best, most expensive eggshell recliners he'd ever been in.

But as advanced as the bed was, its restraints were simple touch-fastened straps, manually tightened. The one around Maddox's left wrist hadn't been secured as snugly as the right one. He hoped it was enough space for him to work with.

As a kid, he and his turfies had once stolen a pair of police handcuffs from a dozing beat cop. They'd made a game out of escaping from them, and no one had been able to do it as well as Maddox. He wasn't sure why—double-jointed thumbs, maybe?—but he'd been able to fold his hands much narrower than his friends could. They'd marveled at his ability to slip out of the cuffs, even at two notches tighter than anyone else's setting.

Lying there, he hoped he remembered the trick of it. He rotated his forearm back and forth and tucked his thumb as far under his palm as he could. To his relief and amazement, in less than a minute his arm was free. He quickly unfastened the other straps, freeing his right arm and both legs, and then he removed the oxygen line from his nose. His head throbbing, he began to swing his legs off the bed but then stopped. If he lost contact with the bed and its embedded biosensors, would it set off an alarm somewhere? He sat there, trying to breathe slow and keep his pulse rate down despite his growing panic. He didn't know where he was, didn't know who'd brought him here or even what had happened. If he hopped off the bed and ran out of the room, he might find a corridor and a nearby emergency exit. He might just as easily find an armed guard right outside the room.

He found it hard to decide on a next move with this head pounding so mercilessly. It wasn't like a headache or a hangover. And it wasn't even like he'd been knocked out, which he had been on several occasions, so he was familiar with the dizzying process of coming to. It felt as if someone were banging on his skull from the inside. The throbbing's epicenter was behind his left ear, and it radiated a dull pain through his entire head. Instinctively, he reached up and touched the spot where the pain was coming from. He felt something.

A small bandage was taped to his head. He gingerly poked at it and winced, finding the skin underneath tender like a bruise. Around the bandage, his skin was smooth where there should have been hair. Someone had shaved a small bald patch behind his ear.

No, he thought, instantly horrified. It can't be. It can't be that.

Ignoring the biomonitor alarms that began chirping the instant he leapt off the bed, Maddox stumbled over to a small mirror on the wall, knocking over the bedside table in the process. He turned to the side and watched his mirrored hand slowly begin to peel away the bandage. He craned his neck as far as it would turn, but from his viewpoint it was impossible to make out what the bandage had covered.

He could feel it well enough, though. He ran his fingertip over the implants, the metal strangely warm like his own flesh. Dropping the bandage to the floor, he gasped, drawing his hand away from the brainjacks and backing away from the mirror.

The door swung open, slamming against the wall. The red-haired woman rushed in, then stopped short as she saw the bandage on the floor and realized what had happened.

Trembling and unable to catch his breath, Maddox swallowed hard and tried to process the horror he'd woken up to. And he *was* awake. This was no nightmare. He was really here, wherever this was, and the unthinkable had really happened. He looked at the woman, his shock and dread already giving way to a surging rage.

He took a menacing step forward and growled, "What the hell did you do to me?"

23
DITCHED

Mixed feelings. Beatrice had come across this two-word phrase countless times. She'd read it in books, heard it spoken on entertainment feeds. A character in a movie wins a race by defeating a friend. The hero of a novel can only save the day by deceiving a loved one. The politicians and corporati she protected for a living used the phrase often, especially when someone was leaving their job. *It's with mixed feelings we're saying goodbye to Joe Blow today, and we wish him all our best in his new endeavors.* Most of the time "mixed feelings" was a bullshit remark, a nice way of saying you didn't like something. *I've got mixed feelings about my cousin's new wife.* Translation: my cousin just married a cunt.

As she and Tommy climbed the stairs and exited the subway onto the bustling streets of Park Avenue West, Beatrice reflected on how woefully inadequate those two words were at expressing the storm raging inside her. There was a part of her that wanted to kick down Lora's door, tie her up, and beat the woman's face bloody until she spilled why her 'Nette brothers and sisters had tried to murder Beatrice on that plane.

Then there was another part of her that didn't want to take another step in the direction of Lora's condo, that didn't want to meet the woman at all. She was the salaryman's ex, and Beatrice had thought of her from time to time over the last couple years, always with an unsettling mix of dread and curiosity. What did she look like? Did she still have feelings for Maddox or had all of that gone away when she'd had the brainjacks installed? Had Beatrice ever come up in their conversations? Did the two of them even have conversations any longer? She laughed inwardly at herself, at the resurgence of the questions anchored in her own self-doubts. She sounded like some foolish woman from a romance movie feed. Beatrice the insecure romantic. What was the world coming to?

Tommy pointed to a graffiti-free building of polished granite a block ahead of them. "That's it right there," he said.

They walked on, both wearing veil specs to conceal their identities from street cams. Tommy still had his pair from the airport, and they'd picked up another for Beatrice from a gear dealer Tommy knew, who operated on the Jersey side of the George Washington Bridge. By now the police had surely taped off the jet as a crime scene, and they'd figured out one of the names from the flight's passenger list wasn't accounted for. Out of caution, she'd traveled using one of her fake passports, and she'd worn an oversized pair of veil specs—the ones she'd since tossed into the Hudson River when Tommy had gotten her a fresh pair—to conceal her face. She was reasonably certain the police couldn't ID her from airport security cam footage, but of course you could never be completely sure about these things. You could also never be sure if something else, like a clever rogue AI, might be tapping into street cam feeds.

As they approached the building, the practical matter of how to gain access began to dominate Beatrice's thoughts. It was a nice building in a wealthy neighborhood. They wouldn't simply be able to stroll in, walk across the lobby, and take the elevator up to Lora's floor. There would be security and check-ins and who knew what kind of surveillance tech scanning them the moment they stepped through the entryway.

As if he'd been reading her thoughts, Tommy said, "Just leave it to me, mama. I'll get us in."

Beatrice wasn't sure if the kid's confidence was street bluster or not, but as reluctant as she was to admit it, whatever the kid had in mind was probably better than anything she might come up with on a moment's notice. Tommy had at least been here before; Beatrice hadn't.

"Just don't do anything that'll call attention to us," she warned.

"No problem," he said, still far too self-assured for her liking.

At the building's arched entryway they found a call screen embedded in the wall. "We have to call up here first," Tommy explained, "then check in at the front desk."

The kid stepped in front of the screen. "Lora Norville, please."

A moment later, the darkened screen blinked to life, and a thirtyish woman appeared. Green eyes, a short bob of chestnut hair, light-skinned, attractive by any standard. So this was Lora.

"Tommy?" she asked. "What can I do for you?" She spoke calmly, and if she was at all surprised to see the kid, nothing in her face betrayed it.

"It's kind of an emergency," he replied. "About Blackburn. We have to talk."

"What kind of emergency?" Lora asked.

The kid glanced up and down the avenue's crowded walkway. "I'd rather not say here out in the open. Can I come up for a minute?"

"Who's that with you?" Lora asked pointedly.

Tommy waved dismissively. "That's just my mom."

"Your mom?" Lora blurted, her eyes widening, though her surprise was nothing compared to Beatrice's. What the hell was the kid thinking? Tommy had managed to impress her on many occasions with his canny street smarts. This was not one of those occasions.

"I'm a friend of Blackburn's," Beatrice said, stepping forward. "Something's happened. We need to speak to you. It's urgent."

There was a moment's hesitation, then Lora said, "I'll buzz you in and tell lobby security to send you right up." As Lora's image blinked away, a green light appeared at the bottom of the screen, accompanied by a tinny buzz. The revolving door began to spin slowly, allowing the pair entry to the building.

Tommy gave Beatrice a sly grin and gestured toward the doorway. "After you, Mother dear."

Beatrice frowned at him. "Not funny, kid," she said, pushing past him. "Not funny at all."

* * *

They checked in at the front desk, leaving the false names that matched those on their specs, and the concierge showed them to the elevator. On the way up, Beatrice wished she hadn't chucked the pistols she'd taken from the pilot and copilot into the Hudson along with her old specs. While she didn't believe she'd need a weapon with Lora, she would have felt more secure armed, especially going into an uncertain situation. But ditching the guns had been the right call, she reminded herself. Carrying around a piece used in a murder, right after you'd entered the country with a fake passport, would have been too much of a gamble. And besides, in an upscale residence like this one, they probably had a weapons detector in the lobby, so there wasn't much point in regretting a lack of firepower.

They exited the elevator on the twenty-second floor. Beatrice pulled Tommy to a stop right before they reached Lora's door, gave him a stern look. "Let me do the talking, yeah?"

Tommy shrugged. "Sure, B. Your party, I get it."

Beatrice knocked on the door and waited. No one answered. She looked at Tommy. "The concierge said 2287, didn't he?"

"That's what he said," Tommy confirmed.

She knocked again. Nothing. "Stay quiet for a second," she told the kid. Then she pressed her ear to the door, closed her eyes, and concentrated.

In the four years since she'd had them put in, she'd rarely had the occasion to use her auditory implants. Most often her work involved settings filled with noisy crowds where ultrasensitive hearing wasn't much of an asset. She'd often regretted investing in the expensive hearing upgrade, having put it to so little use over the years. But every once in a long while, enhanced hearing came in handy. Like when you wanted to know the contents of an otherwise inaudible conversation across a large room, or like now, when you needed to know if there was someone on the other side of a door or not.

After a long moment, Beatrice opened her eyes. "Either she's perfectly still or she's not in there." She looked down the corridor. There was only one elevator for this floor, and she and Tommy had monopolized it for the last few moments, so if Maddox's ex had ditched them, it hadn't been by taking the elevator.

Already thinking along the same lines, Tommy pushed through the stairwell door. Poking his head back into the corridor, he said, "Can't see who it is, but somebody's five flights up, and climbing fast."

"Go down and watch the lobby in case she takes the elevator from another floor," Beatrice told him as she hurried into the stairwell. "Call me if you see her."

"On it," Tommy said, disappearing back into the corridor.

Alone in the stairwell, Beatrice paused to listen as she looked up into the gap between the flights of stairs. She caught a glimpse of a blurred silhouette on a landing half a dozen floors up, heard a rapid click-clack of heels on cement stairs. If it was Lora up there, she was in one hell of a hurry. Beatrice grabbed the handrail and propelled herself up the stairs. Taking each flight in three lunging steps, she soon cut the distance in half. At each landing she'd take another glance up, but she couldn't get a clean look.

Then, just as she'd nearly caught up, her prey suddenly disappeared. Beatrice paused at the next landing, breathing heavily from the upward sprint and debating which floor's corridor to check first, this one or the one above. Then she heard the soft click of a door latch and turned her head instinctively toward the sound. She rushed forward and opened the door, stepping through into a hover vestibule, where Lora was climbing into a waiting vehicle. She looked back at Beatrice with wide eyes as she hit the door control. Beatrice bolted for the hover as the door began to slide downward, then stuck her arm through the narrow gap at the last moment. A safety alarm chirped as the door stopped then opened wide again. Grabbing Lora by the arm, Beatrice yanked her from the hover and hustled her over to the doorway to the corridor.

"Not the warmest welcome, ditching us like that," she said.

"Let go of me!" Lora cried, trying to break the mercenary's grip. "I'll call security."

"You do that," Beatrice said. "And then how about we show them our upgrades? They'll like my eyes, but something tells me they'll be much more interested in what you've got there behind your ear."

Lora stopped struggling and fixed Beatrice with a cold, menacing stare. "What is it you want?"

"Like the kid said," Beatrice replied, "we need to talk." She tapped her specs, calling Tommy. "I've got her. Meet me back at her place."

Beatrice released the woman's arm. "Come on, let's go."

"And what if I don't feel like talking to you?" Lora snapped, rubbing her arm where Beatrice had gripped it.

"Then maybe you'll talk with me," a voice said.

Both women whirled around in surprise, finding a man pointing a gun at them.

24
CONFESSION

In Beatrice's everyday work, she carried a firearm as a precaution, but in the years she'd spent in the security business, she'd only had to take it out a handful of times. And even less frequent were the occasions when a gun had been pointed in her direction. Her involvement with Maddox and a psychotic AI had changed all that. Over the last couple years, she'd lost track of how many times she'd been shot at by police and brainjacked 'Nettes and hired thugs. And although the proud mercenary in her wanted to believe it was her skill and cunning that had saved her, she couldn't deny that she'd had more than her fair share of luck. And since the short middle-aged man who stood before her was the third person today who'd held a gun on her, she began to wonder if her luck had finally run out.

Two suited men in dark specs flanked the gun-wielding man. Maybe hotel security, maybe thugs hired by whoever this squat, disheveled man was.

The man turned back toward the corridor, waving Beatrice and Lora forward with the gun. "Come, ladies. Let's have a chat, shall we?"

*   *   *

Nakedfaced, their lenses confiscated, Beatrice and Lora exited the stairwell on Lora's floor. Tommy was already there, a few doors down, waiting for them. The kid's grin of recognition faded into confusion at the three men who appeared behind the two women. The kid furrowed his brow and squinted at the man with the gun. "Kipling? What are you doing here?"

"I might ask you the same question, young man," the man replied.

Beatrice shifted her gaze between them. "Wait, you two know each other?"

"He's a highfloor FBI man," Tommy said. "He was in D.C. with me and Maddox." The kid looked at the gun. "He was a lot nicer this morning, though."

FBI? Now Beatrice was more confused than ever. How was the FBI wrapped up in this mess? She gave Tommy a what-the-hell look.

The kid's expression turned sheepish. "Oh, man, did I forget to tell you about the FBI stuff?"

"Yes," Beatrice said, "you kind of did."

The man Tommy called Kipling ushered them into Lora's condo. He took the kid's specs, handed them to one of his companions, who both then exited the residence and stationed themselves outside the door. "Please, have a seat," he said. When the two women and Tommy sat, Kipling returned his gun to a shoulder holster inside his jacket, then he took a seat across from them. He fixed Tommy with a stern gaze.

"Why didn't you get on that plane to Toronto?" he asked.

The kid fidgeted the way he always did when he was caught doing something he shouldn't. "I've got biz in the City," he answered, shrugging. "Can't just up and leave it, you know."

Kipling looked between the kid and Beatrice. "And why did you two come here?" he asked, though Beatrice wasn't sure if the question was directed at Tommy or her.

Beatrice didn't answer. She wasn't about to go down that path with this stranger. Tommy kept his mouth shut as well.

The FBI man didn't wait long for a reply. He had the impatient, slightly irritable manner of someone accustomed to having his questions answered quickly and completely. Reaching into his jacket pocket, he removed his FBI credentials—a small leather badge holder, a plastic card inside with his photo and the FBI seal—and showed them to the trio.

"My name is Stellan Kipling and I run the data crimes division of the Federal Bureau of Investigation." He paused for a moment, letting the weight of his title sink in. "This would go a lot quicker if you simply told me the truth." He returned the holder to his pocket without breaking his gaze from Beatrice. "Now, tell me why you're here."

Beatrice pondered her response. With all the leverage tilted in the FBI man's favor, she quickly surmised there was no choice but to answer him. This Kipling fellow could ruin her life in less than a minute, if only by busting her for the forged IDs on the specs he'd taken from her. Still, given what happened, full disclosure didn't seem like a wise option either. Not with so much blood on her hands.

"I needed to talk with her," she said, tilting her head toward Lora, who sat silently with Tommy between them.

"About what?" Kipling pressed. "What exactly?"

"Some of her friends," Beatrice answered carefully, "were giving me a hard time. I wanted to know why."

Kipling narrowed his eyes. "A hard time meaning…?"

"Let's just say I had an unpleasant run-in with them."

The FBI man lifted his eyebrows. "An unpleasant run-in?"

"Right. And they weren't inclined to tell me what it was about, so I thought she might know." Beatrice felt as if she were slowly sinking in mud, unable to free herself. Maybe she should just shut up and ask for a lawyer. But that might only anger this Kipling and make things worse.

"And did she know?" he asked.

"You showed up before we got around to it," Beatrice said.

Kipling took a long breath before continuing. "Very well. We'll sort out all the details later. At the moment I've got more pressing matters to attend to. Blackburn Maddox's whereabouts, for instance. Do you know where he is?" The question seemed to be directed at all three of them. Moments passed, but no one answered.

"I'll give you each one more opportunity to answer," Kipling said, adjusting his specs. "And whoever chooses not to tell the truth will have to leave this lovely building in handcuffs."

He asked Tommy first. "Where is Blackburn Maddox?"

"I don't know," the kid said.

Next, he turned to Beatrice. "Do you know where Maddox is?"

She shook her head. "I don't have any idea."

Last was Lora. "And you, Ms. Norville? Would you happen to know Blackburn Maddox's current whereabouts?"

Beatrice glanced over at Maddox's ex. The woman sat there with her hands folded on her lap and a serene, impossibly calm expression on her face. "No, I don't," she replied smoothly.

A slow smile spread across Beatrice's face. "She's lying," she muttered to herself. Then she turned to Kipling and said in a normal tone, "She's lying."

Kipling nodded, adjusting his specs. "Yes, I know she is."

"I'm not," Lora protested, suddenly flustered. "I swear I don't know—"

"Please, Ms. Norville," Kipling interrupted, waving her silent. "Don't waste any more of my time. Every minute is crucial right now." He removed his specs and tucked them into the buttonhole on his lapel. "I was scheduled to meet Maddox and one of my agents at a cafe across the street. We were coming to ask you some questions related to an investigation. Maddox and my agent never showed up, and I'm unable to reach either one of them. They've both gone missing."

A few pieces came together for Beatrice. "So when the kid and I showed up, you saw us and followed us in."

"I did," Kipling said. He then turned once more to Lora. "Now, tell me where Maddox is."

"I…I…," she stammered. "I can't—"

"Your life of keeping secrets is over, Ms. Norville," Kipling said, his voice raised. "No more secrets about Maddox, about your rogue AI benefactor, about those implants behind your ear."

Beatrice and Tommy gasped in unison. Kipling knew! He knew about Lora, about the 'Nettes and their AI master. Had Maddox sold her out? Had he cut a deal to save his skin? Lora's face twisted with frozen horror, her mouth hanging open. She covered her face with her hands and shook her head.

"Oh my God, my God," she cried. "Blackburn, what have you done?" Then to Kipling: "What did he tell you?"

"Tell me where he is!" the FBI man insisted, rising to his feet.

"I didn't want them to do it," Lora sobbed, tears flowing down her cheeks. "I told them it was wrong to force it on him."

"Do what?" Kipling pressed.

"I told them not to do it," Lora repeated, now weeping uncontrollably.

Kipling approached her and gripped her by the shoulders. "Do what?" he asked. "Do what to him?"

She turned her gaze upward, her eyes wet and shining. "They connected him to us."

25
ROOFTOP

Maddox didn't know what the red-haired woman's role was at this clinic or off-grid surgery center or whatever this place was. Maybe she was the surgeon who'd implanted these fucking things into his head. Or maybe she'd had nothing at all to do with the procedure, and she was only a recovery nurse. But at that moment he didn't care whether or not she'd had a direct hand in brainjacking him. All that mattered was that she was part of whoever or whatever had brought him here, and she was standing between him and his escape. As she stood there, still gawking at him in disbelief, he lunged forward and landed a sharp hook to the point of her chin. She crumpled to the floor, knocked out cold.

He then searched the room, finding his clothes in a plastic bin under the bed. Quickly, he changed out of the surgical gown back into his own shirt, pants, and shoes. Leaning down, he removed the woman's specs from her face and tucked them into his shirt pocket. Then he moved to the door, and as slowly and quietly as he could, he turned and pulled on the knob. He'd expected to find at least one armed guard standing outside, but there was no one there. The corridor was empty and quiet. He padded out of the room, relieved to find the exit sign for the stairwell only a few meters away.

"Where do you think you're going?" a voice behind him called out. Looking over, Maddox saw a large, muscled man in a sleeveless shirt exiting the restroom a few doors down. He wore a shoulder holster in plain sight, and as he reached for his handgun, he barked, "Stay right there."

The datajacker bolted for the stairwell, ignoring the man's repeated shouts, expecting to hear a gunshot at any moment. He strode up the stairs clumsily, his legs feeling less like his own limbs than two unwieldy logs attached to his body. The aftereffects of the anesthesia, he realized. His mind was awake and alert, but his body hadn't caught up yet.

Then he realized he'd gone *up* the stairs instead of down. Why had he done that? Maybe he hadn't shaken all the post-surgery cobwebs after all. As he reached the next floor's landing, the door he'd gone through a floor below burst open, and the armed man rushed into the stairwell. Going back down now wasn't an option, unless he wanted to get shot. He paused for a moment, hoping his pursuer would assume the datajacker had taken a downward escape route. Peeking over the rail, Maddox saw the man tearing down the stairs, chasing after his invisible prey. Less panicked now, Maddox began to climb again, taking the steps at a hurried but measured pace, stepping carefully so he didn't make any noise. A few flights later, he reached the thirty-second floor, apparently the top level, since there were no more upward stairs. A door with the words HOVER ACCESS above it stood before him. The building's rooftop landing pad, his best and probably only chance for escape, lay beyond the door. Far below him, he heard the sounds of his pursuer, steadily fading. The man was still going the wrong way.

He took out the woman's specs and started for the door. There were tens of thousands of automated private hovers in the City, tirelessly moving through the traffic stacks day and night, waiting for customers to ping them via ride apps in their specs. All he had to do was reboot the woman's specs, select a temporary user ID, then pull up a ride app.

Pushing through the door, he found he wasn't alone. At the center of the wide rooftop, a hover lifted skyward in the drizzling rain, then turned away from Maddox and began to slide forward toward the transit lane. The vehicle's drop-off passenger strode toward Maddox with his head down, apparently unaware of the datajacker's presence as he lifted his trench coat collar against the falling rain. In the small moment Maddox took to consider where he might hide himself—either back in the stairwell or behind the large ductwork of a nearby exhaust vent—the man lifted his head into view. Both men froze as they recognized each other.

"Nguyen," Maddox gasped. What was he doing here? Had the agent come here to kill him?

Behind Maddox, the door he'd passed through a moment before burst open. His pursuer appeared, pistol in hand and breathing heavily. The man saw Nguyen and stopped cold, his suddenly uncertain gaze shifting between Maddox and the agent.

"What did I tell you?" Nguyen called over to the armed man. "Total waste of time hooking him up."

"Let me handle this," the bald man shouted, "I've got it under control."

Nguyen shook his head reproachfully and approached the man. "Like hell you do. It took him, what, all of five minutes to ditch you? Christ, I'm glad I never hired you over at the Bureau." He snatched the pistol from the man's hand. "You all should have listened to me. I guess that's pretty obvious now, isn't it?" He lifted his chin toward the door. "Go on, I'll handle this."

The man stood there, still catching his breath, his expression crestfallen like some berated child. After a moment, he turned away and left the two men alone on the rooftop.

The agent grinned. "You should see the look on your face, jacker."

Maddox swallowed, then reached up and touched the implants behind his ear. "They put brainjacks in me," he said, though he began to suspect this was hardly news to the agent.

"Wasn't my idea, believe me," Nguyen said. He glanced down at the pistol in his hand. "My solution was a much simpler one."

"Tell me, Nguyen," Maddox said. "Tell me what the hell is going on."

Nguyen stepped closer. "You know more than enough already. And that's the whole problem." Beyond the agent, the transit lanes moved sluggishly in the hazy distance. The rain came down heavier now, in large drops that thudded against the building's roof, drowning out the whine of the distant hover motors and forming puddles here and there.

Again, Nguyen flashed Maddox an unsettling smile. "I will tell you one thing before you die, although I'm not sure it'll clear anything up for you."

Maddox's eyes dropped to the gun. He took a step backward. "And what's that?"

Nguyen turned his head to one side, and with his free hand he peeled away a skin-colored patch from behind his ear, revealing his own brainjacks.

Then he raised the pistol toward Maddox. "Welcome to the family, brother."

26
GRIM RIDE

"Brainjacks," Tommy muttered to himself. He still didn't want to believe what Lora had confessed back at the condo, didn't want to picture Maddox with those things drilled into his head. His teacher and friend, brain-raped and forced to become a 'Nette. It was like some terrible waking nightmare.

From the back seat of the FBI hover, he stared out the window, its paned glass streaked with raindrops, watching the City's mountainous hiverises pass by. The overcast sky cast a gray gloom over everything, dulling the otherwise colorful graffiti skins of the buildings' lowfloor sections. Even the enormous holo ads, normally eye-catching and brilliant, seemed uncharacteristically drab and flat.

"We don't know that they actually went through with it," Beatrice said, trying to comfort him.

"I know," Tommy said, but agreeing with her didn't make him feel any better. He hated how he'd left things with Maddox, storming out on him like that. Maybe the old man was just looking out for him, trying to keep him out of trouble. But when you were in trouble, real trouble, you didn't push your friends away, especially if they wanted to help out. Hell, that was when you needed friends the most, wasn't it? The truest friends jumped into the fire with you, no questions asked, just like his turfies, the Anarchy Boyz, always did. Only a few nights ago, Tommy had pushed Maddox out of the way of a kamikaze hover that surely would've killed him. If that didn't prove to the man he was better off with Tommy Park around, what would? But the old man was nothing if not stubborn, and he'd been determined to send the kid away. Still, Tommy cursed himself for bailing on him so easily. He should have insisted on sticking around. If he had, maybe he could have kept the old man from getting brainjacked.

"We'll be there in ten minutes," the driver said.

Back at the condo, Lora, sobbing uncontrollably, had given up the location of the clandestine clinic where her fellow 'Nettes had taken Maddox. When pressed as to why her companions had wanted to "connect" Maddox to their AI overlord against his will, she'd had no answer. Through tears she explained that moments before Tommy and Beatrice had arrived, a close friend of hers—a neurally implanted sister who worked at the clinic—had called, telling Lora that her ex was prepped for neural implant surgery. Familiar with Lora's and Maddox's personal histories, the friend had believed it strange someone like Maddox, who according to Lora loathed their sacred movement, would have had such a sudden and complete change of heart. Curious as to his reasons, she'd called Lora to ask what had changed his mind. At first Lora had believed the call to be a prank, but once she'd realized it was nothing of the sort, she'd pleaded with the friend to intervene, to stop the procedure. She knew Maddox never would have consented to neural implants. Never in a million years. Her friend, a newly connected member of the order and worried about making waves, had apparently chosen not to intercede. Lora had been about to call the clinic and raise hell when Tommy and Beatrice's arrival had interrupted her.

To Kipling's frustration, Lora knew nothing of his missing agent. Impatient to follow up on the lead, the FBI man left Lora in the custody of his two agents, hustling Tommy and Beatrice out of the condo and into a waiting hover.

Now they were on their way to this secret clinic where wannabe 'Nettes got their brainjacks installed, the tech that hooked them into their AI goddess. From what Tommy had learned from Maddox, once you were connected by brainjacks, there was no thought the entity couldn't access, no biofunction it couldn't monitor. When you were a 'Nette, you willingly turned yourself over to the cybernetic, body, mind, and soul. True believers like Lora claimed the act was one of liberation. Their AI-assisted life maximized their happiness, enabling Lora and her 'Nette brothers and sisters to make the right decisions about work and companionship, about where to live and how to spend money, about which clothes to wear. The one with whom they were connected—that was how they referred to their beloved AI, a reference Tommy always found creepy—also helped them overcome their own self-destructive nature or any harmful habits rooted in what Maddox had called "the bad chemistry of their meat sacks." Like a datajacker tweaking an app's default settings, the

'Nette's AI made adjustments to its followers' neurochemistry. Lessening a smoker's predisposition for addiction, for example, or bolstering endorphin output for someone with depressive tendencies.

For the 'Nette faithful, this new way of life was nothing short of personal salvation, but theirs was a fringe movement, a cult of AI fanatics. For the vast majority of the general public, the idea of a superintelligent machine with tendrils reaching into your mind was appalling in the extreme. Even before brainjacks had been invented, AIs had become widely loathed as job stealers, soulless destroyers of countless occupations, having over the last century supplanted human labor on a scale never seen before in human history. Despite the inarguable benefits AIs had brought humankind—death by cancer had been all but eliminated, for example—intelligent machines were far more hated for what they'd taken away than they were loved for what they'd brought. Sharing the public's wariness and skepticism, politicians and lawmakers—in the US and around the world—had outlawed AI-enabled neural implants, effectively forcing the 'Nette movement underground. For the last decade, the 'Nettes' infinitely clever AI goddess had managed to keep her movement's existence secret, its list of names hidden from view. But now it seemed all of that was coming to an end.

The nuances of the movement's goals and ideals were lost on Tommy. All he cared about was that its founding entity, the rogue AI that had appeared to Maddox on a windswept virtual beach, had messed with his friends' lives. And with his life too. And now apparently it was planning to force brain mods on Maddox, if it hadn't already done so. That was so messed up. So seriously messed up.

"Are we under arrest?" Beatrice asked the FBI man, breaking a prolonged silence.

"Not at the moment," Kipling replied. "I wanted to finish our conversation, and I thought we could use the time in transit to do that." He adjusted his specs. "Now, tell me why you were there. And this time don't leave anything out."

Beatrice didn't answer, saying instead, "You have no idea what you're up against."

Kipling blinked purposefully and moved his lips without speaking, the way people did sometimes when they subvocalized. The FBI man was preoccupied with some unseen task in his specs. A few moments later, his attention returned to Beatrice. "You're absolutely right, I don't. That's why I had a dozen agents secure Ms. Norville's building a few moments ago. And when we arrive at this clinic, another dozen will meet us there." He grinned mischievously and added, "Apparently, the local Bureau chief isn't terribly pleased with how I've monopolized a large portion of his agent pool on a moment's notice. I suppose I'll have to mend a bridge or two when all of this is over."

He settled back into his seat. "So you're not in the mood to chat, I take it?"

Beatrice remained silent and turned to gaze out the window.

"All right, then," he said, "have it your way for now. But later we'll talk in much more detail about a great many things. Like an abandoned aircraft in New Jersey. And the five bodies found inside, all of them with strange implants behind their ears. And the security cam feeds from Toronto Pearson's charter terminal, where someone who looks a great deal like you boarded a flight for D.C. that never reached its destination."

Again, the mischievous grin appeared. "But we can talk about all of that later, when you're in the mood, yes?"

27
LEDGE

Surprising a datajacker wasn't easy. In their illicit profession, the astounding was commonplace, the surreal ordinary. When you were plugged into core virtual space, deep inside the pulsing center of a datasphere, information visualized as flowing rivers of dazzling light. Security programs were neon crabs crawling across the luminescent surfaces of data partitions. Your jacking tools might visualize as a cartoon hammer or a purple mist you unleashed like some horror movie monster. And you had no body. You were ethereal, one with the digital, a cybernetic god capable of unimaginable feats. The real world, in contrast, was drab and mundane, a place where you were constrained by the animal limitations of your meat sack. For most datajackers, the boring, predictable nature of reality offered comparatively little in the way of thrills or the unexpected.

Until these last few minutes, Maddox had believed that his ability to be surprised had long since been exhausted. But since the moment he'd stirred to consciousness in the recovery bed, he'd been hit with one heart-stopping shock after another, and this last was perhaps the wildest of all.

Special Agent Alex Nguyen was a 'Nette.

Nguyen waved the gun. "Move away from the door." Maddox circled away from both the door and Nguyen, reflexively distancing himself from the lethal weapon trained on him.

Still reeling, Maddox asked, "Why did you brainjack me? And why even go to the trouble if you're just going to kill me?"

A predator stalking prey, Nguyen stepped forward with deadly intent behind his eyes. "We make the brain perfect before we blow it out."

"How does that make any sense?" Maddox asked, backing up another step.

"It doesn't, really," Nguyen said. "Just something I read once. Struck me as appropriate for the occasion." He continued moving toward the datajacker. Maddox matched him, taking one step back for each Nguyen took forward. Then his heel struck against something hard. He flailed slightly, nearly tripping over backwards, but he managed to stay on his feet. Glancing behind him, he found he'd reached the rooftop's ledge. Far below, the street went about its business, indifferent to his plight. Lights flashing in dazzling neon, crowds flowing like blood through the City's arteries.

When he looked back to Nguyen, he found the menace in the agent's expression replaced with a kind of distracted confusion. The man had stopped moving forward, and his gaze had moved to some point beyond Maddox.

"No, we should have done this a long time ago," Nguyen said, apparently to no one, then blinked impatiently as if he were listening. It was like he'd received a call in his specs, except at the moment he wasn't wearing any lenses.

The nameless AI, Maddox realized. That had to be who—what—Nguyen was talking to.

"It has to be done," Nguyen said, his gaze returning to Maddox, "for the good of us all. Can't you see that?"

Nguyen lifted the gun, leveling it at Maddox's midsection. Time slowed for Maddox, the way it sometimes did in virtual space. In the time it took to blink, so many thoughts raced through his mind. Things he regretted, mostly. The nagging guilt over Rooney's end, always there, never diminished. He wouldn't live to set things right, to destroy Rooney's killer once and for all. And he hated how he'd left things with Tommy, how their last words had been harsh ones. Tommy was a good kid, with a good soul. He'd seen the worst depravity the City had to offer, and it hadn't crushed his spirit like it had with so many others. It hadn't jaded him. What an amazing person that noodle-eating kid was. And what a shame it was that Maddox only now fully realized it.

And then there was Beatrice. How utterly and completely he'd messed that up. She'd reached out to him, made herself vulnerable to him—more than once—and he'd stupidly pushed her away. What a fool he'd been. What a bloody fool.

He felt the top of the building's ledge pressed against his rear. The street was thirty stories below. All he had to do was lean backwards and let himself fall. If something had to take his life in the next few moments, he'd rather let the street do it than this damned 'Nette.

Don't do it, boyo.

Sorry, Roon.

The decision made, he began to lean back when the stairwell door flew open behind Nguyen.

"Stop, please!" a metallic voice cried.

Nguyen turned away from Maddox. A robot stood in the doorway. Five feet tall, the bot's two-armed, two-legged body was covered in polished chrome plating. It was the kind of expensive-looking bot Maddox associated with the highfloor wealthy, who often used such models as in-home servants to cook meals, clean up after them, and do other menial chores.

"Alex, don't do this," the robot said, stepping forward into the rain.

"You," Maddox said. "It's you, isn't it?"

The bot stopped, briefly shifting its gaze to the datajacker. "Yes, my dear boy."

"This has to be done!" Nguyen shouted. "For the good of us all!"

Rushing forward, the bot reached for Nguyen, but the agent easily dodged the machine's grasping hands. Service robots were neither quick nor agile. They were designed to be helpers, not fighters. Maddox recalled how kids often toppled them over for fun when they came across one running an errand for its owner.

Nguyen lunged forward, landing a powerful kick to the bot's midsection, sending it sprawling across the rooftop. The downed robot lay in a puddle, its arms and legs flailing like an overturned turtle. Nguyen turned back to Maddox and raised the pistol.

"Goodbye, jacker," Nguyen said, and in the next moment the agent's forehead exploded. Frozen in place, Maddox couldn't comprehend what had happened as he watched Nguyen collapse to the rooftop, the gaping wound in his head spurting blood into a rainwater puddle. The agent's body twitched grotesquely, then went still.

In the stairwell doorway stood Kipling, a small pistol in his raised hand, the barrel still smoking. He lowered the weapon, walked over to Agent Nguyen, and shook his head. Behind Kipling, still in the doorway, were Beatrice and Tommy. They looked as surprised as Maddox felt at that moment. Then suddenly there were blaring sirens everywhere, and hovers with flashing red and blue lights surrounded the building.

Kipling knelt down beside Nguyen and grasped the dead man's chin, moving his head to one side. He nodded to himself as he spied the brainjacks. Then he looked over at Maddox.

"I never really liked Agent Nguyen," he said. "There was something about him that always struck me the wrong way. Now I suppose I know what that something was."

Forgetting his brainjacks for a moment, Maddox let out a relieved breath. Then he noticed Kipling seemed unaware of the bot lying in a puddle a few meters away. The white whale he'd been chasing for years was here on the roof with him.

Maddox gestured. "The bot over there," he told Kipling. "The nameless AI's driving it."

Kipling furrowed his brow. "What bot?" He pivoted around just as the machine regained its feet, its chrome plating wet and gleaming.

"We'll talk soon, Blackburn," the AI said.

Kipling sprung to his feet. "No, please wait!" But

the AI was already gone. The bot's body collapsed into a powerless heap as its unseen puppeteer severed the connection.

28
LOYAL FRIENDS

His head still throbbing, Maddox sat with Beatrice on a sofa across from Kipling, seated in a chair. The medic, a 'Nette whose office they'd taken over, had been taken into custody and marched out of the building a minute earlier. A man and woman, both with large automatic rifles slung over their shoulders, stood guard outside the door. Beyond the room, the door-busting frenzy of the building-wide raid had begun to wind down. Dozens had been arrested, according to Kipling. At least fifteen 'Nettes among them.

Kipling shook his head in disappointment. "This wasn't the way it was supposed to be."

"How do you mean?" Maddox asked.

The FBI man smiled faintly. "I'd always imagined the day my supposedly crazy theories were vindicated would be a celebratory one. But it doesn't quite feel that way." Again he shook his head. "My own department infiltrated," the FBI man said, more to himself than Maddox. "Never in my wildest dreams did I imagine such a thing was possible."

Tommy appeared in the doorway, but the female guard stopped the kid with a firm hand on his shoulder. Kipling waved her off. "It's all right," he told her, and she let the kid enter.

He tossed a bag of tobacco to Maddox. "They had your brand in the shop next door."

"Thanks, kid," Maddox said, unfolding the bag, removing the rolling papers, and letting his hands go through the automatic motion of rolling a smoke.

"Brought you this, too," Tommy said, proffering a small gauze bandage. "You know," he said awkwardly, "so you can cover up…" The kid's voice trailed off, leaving the rest of the sentence unspoken.

Maddox stared at the bandage and didn't say anything. After a long moment, Beatrice said, "Here, I'll do it." She took the bandage from Maddox's hand and removed the adhesive's backing.

"Turn your head a little to the right," she said. Maddox instead turned to his left, toward Beatrice, and studied her face. What was she thinking right now? Was she disgusted by him? Fearful of him? He felt as if he'd been transformed into some hideous monster and that neither she nor Tommy would never look at him the same way again.

"It's all right," she said, laying her hand on his arm and gently squeezing. "Let me put it on, Blackburn."

The concern in her expression and the way she said his name broke something inside him. Tears burst forth and flowed down his cheeks. Embarrassed, he quickly wiped them away with his sleeve and turned away from her so she could put the bandage on. What had he ever done in his miserable life to deserve such devotion and kindness? From her, from the kid?

A long quiet moment passed as Maddox finished rolling his cigarette and lit the tip. He inhaled deeply, half-expecting a voice in his head that wasn't Rooney's to admonish him for smoking.

"How do you feel?" Kipling said, leaning forward.

"I have a headache," Maddox replied flatly, but he knew it wasn't the answer Kipling was looking for. "But aside from that," he added, "nothing. There's no AI whispering to me, no sense of…connectedness."

"Then maybe it didn't work," Tommy said hopefully.

"More likely there's a convalescence period," Kipling suggested, dousing the kid's momentary optimism. "Your brain needs to heal up a bit, perhaps, before you can be…" The FBI man had trouble finding the right words.

"Integrated," Maddox said, blowing smoke.

"Yes," Kipling said.

Beatrice stood, then grabbed Kipling by the upper arm and roughly pulled the man to his feet. "What are you doing?" the FBI man protested as she spun him around by the shoulders and placed her hand atop his head, shoving his chin downward into his chest. The two guards rushed into the room and raised their weapons.

"Let go of him, now!" the male guard shouted, but Beatrice ignored the command, running her hand roughly over the back of Kipling's head. Maddox then realized what she was doing, apparently at the same moment Kipling did too. The FBI man thrust his arms outward, palms out in the universal gesture for stop.

"Stand down," he cried to the guards, "it's all right. It's fine, it's fine."

Seemingly satisfied with what she found—or rather what she hadn't found—on Kipling's skull, Beatrice released the director.

"Sorry," she said, though her tone and expression were anything but apologetic. "But I'm sure you understand."

Kipling turned to face her, rubbing the back of his neck. "Yes," he said, then he looked at her dubiously. "I can't say I blame you for being suspicious. But you might have simply asked to see first."

"Again, sorry," she said evenly.

Kipling sent the two guards back to their posts outside the room.

"So what now?" Tommy asked.

The FBI man blew out a breath. "Now, I suppose I owe you a favor, Mr. Maddox. That was our agreement, was it not?"

Maddox smoked, amazed at having temporarily forgotten why he'd come to the FBI for help in the first place. Since he'd woken up with brainjacks, the horror of his new implants had pushed the Latour-Fisher entity from this mind.

"Yes, that was our agreement," Maddox said, "but—"

"Now, it may take me a week or two before I can dedicate myself to it," Kipling said, cutting Maddox off. "Sorting out everything that's happened here today is going to monopolize my time and energy for a good while. But I promise you, I'll use every resource at my disposal to help you with your problem."

"Thanks," Maddox said, then he gave Beatrice a quick glance. She nodded at him assuredly, as if she were confirming the truthfulness of the man's words.

Then to Kipling he said, "But first I want to get these things out of my head." After a short pause, he added, "And I want to do it now."

The FBI man frowned. "You just had brain surgery, Mr. Maddox. I doubt it's safe to undergo another procedure until you've fully recovered."

"I don't feel like waiting." He shifted his gaze to Beatrice. "You know of any off-grid medics around here who could deal with this?"

Beatrice furrowed her brow. "Whoever did this to you is in custody right now. We can just twist their arm, make them reverse what they did."

"I'm afraid that's not possible," Kipling said. "The two medics who performed the procedure shot themselves before we could apprehend them. Perhaps to prevent Mr. Maddox from taking that very course of action."

Maddox nodded grimly, not surprised by the news. From personal experience, he knew 'Nettes were zealots. Even if they'd caught the medics alive, it was doubtful they could be coerced into reversing what they'd done. Not that he'd really want them to try, anyway. The idea of going under the knife again, of making himself vulnerable to those crazies, didn't sit well with him.

"Maybe Wallbrink in Brooklyn," Beatrice offered. "If there's anyone who might know how to help, it's her."

Maddox stood. "Give her a call, would you? Tell her we're on our way."

"Wait a minute," Kipling protested. The raised voice prompted the guards to cast wary glances into the room. "You can't simply leave. You're a material witness to a major ongoing investigation." The FBI man looked at Maddox, Tommy, and Beatrice in turn. "All of you are."

Tommy stepped forward, placing himself between Maddox and Kipling. "Hey, highfloor man," he sneered. "My jefe just got you the biggest bust of your career, didn't he? Maybe you ought to be a little more flexible."

Also taking a step forward, Beatrice added, "That's right. You either owe him or you don't. So which is it?"

Kipling looked between Beatrice and Tommy, then gave Maddox a small grin. "You've got some very loyal friends, Mr. Maddox."

"Seems like I do," Maddox said.

"Very well, then," Kipling said. "If your mind is set, I won't try to dissuade you or stand in your way. And I can't say I blame you. I'd want those things out as soon as possible too if I were in your position." Then he lifted up a forefinger and added, "But I have to insist on sending protection with you. You are still a wanted man, Mr. Maddox. If not by the authorities, then by other parties."

Maddox couldn't deny the man had a point. He nodded toward the two guards. "You want to send those two?"

"Yes," Kipling said, "and myself. Is that acceptable?"

As he had before, the datajacker recognized the man's question as a mere formality, the mannerly habit of a polite individual. Maddox had no power here; both men knew he was in no position to refuse the request. But even if he could have, Maddox reflected, he wouldn't have told the man no. Kipling had just saved his life by shooting one of his own subordinates. No small thing, that. If anyone owed anyone here, Maddox admitted inwardly, it was he who was indebted to Kipling, rather than the other way around.

He nodded at the FBI man. "More than acceptable."

29
JAMMING THE JACKS

Night had settled over the City by the time the FBI hover touched down onto the rooftop of the off-grid clinic in Brooklyn. The ride over had been a quiet one. Seated beside Beatrice, Maddox had stared out at the City's ever-wakeful churn of people and lights and movement. Tommy and Kipling sat on the next bench seat, and in the front row was their security escort.

"If anyone can fix it," Beatrice had said minutes earlier, squeezing his hand, "Wallbrink can. She's just about the best around."

"Then why haven't I ever heard of her?" Maddox asked dejectedly.

"Because she's out of your price range," Beatrice said, but her attempted joke fell flat. After that, they hadn't spoken for the rest of the ride over.

Wearing a white lab coat and flanked by two assistants in blue medical scrubs, the medic greeted them as they exited the vehicle. Tall, light-skinned, and blue-eyed, Wallbrink looked remarkably cool and composed for a proprietor whose illegal clinic had just received an unexpected visit from the FBI.

"Audie Wallbrink," she said, shaking hands all around and leading the four visitors and their security escort down the stairwell. Minutes later, Maddox sat on a padded patient bench in a large, lavishly decorated examination room. Beatrice had been right, he reflected, as he looked around at the expensive-looking equipment, none of which he recognized, and the upscale furniture that looked like it belonged less in a clinic than in the topfloor condo of some wealthy corporati. Dr. Wallbrink's practice was definitely out of his price range.

"Now, let's take a look at you," the medic said, her tone professional and even. "If you could lie back with your head right here on this cushion."

Maddox complied, and Wallbrink made a small hand gesture at the edge of the bench. The datajacker then felt a slight vibration under his head, and on the ceiling above him a small rectangle began to glow faintly. "You can breathe normally," Wallbrink said, "but try to stay as still as possible."

She moved over to a small machine, above which a meter-wide holo display blinked to life. In the edge of his vision, he could see her finger-swiping through one image after another. Tommy, Beatrice, and Kipling looked on from a wide leather sofa next to the wall.

"Have you ever," Kipling said hesitantly, "seen a patient like him before?"

"You mean a 'Nette who wanted their brainjacks removed?" Wallbrink asked without taking her eyes off the display.

"He's not a 'Nette," Tommy growled.

"Yes, yes," the medic said quickly, "my apologies.

You did tell me the implants had been forced on your friend here." She narrowed her eyes at one of the images, then spread her fingers, increasing the resolution. "To answer your question, no, I've never treated a 'Ne…someone with AI-enabled neural implants before. Don't know anyone who has, come to think of it."

"Does that mean you can't help him?" Kipling asked pointedly.

"No," the medic replied without hesitation, "not at all." She smiled and swiped to another image. "There's nothing I love more than a good challenge."

The optimism those words sparked in Maddox died an hour later, when the medic returned to the exam room after finishing her analysis. Her grim expression told Maddox everything he needed to know, even before she began to speak.

"It doesn't look good, I'm afraid," Wallbrink announced, addressing the room.

"Meaning what?" Maddox asked. "You can't remove them?"

"Not without a significant risk of brain damage," she said. "To put it simply, they appear to be designed as permanent implants. Removal—or at least *safe* removal—doesn't seem possible, at least as far as I understand the technology, which admittedly is far beyond anything I've ever dealt with. And from the research I've reviewed, it doesn't look like anyone else has either." Then she added, "Aside from the medics who implanted them, of course."

Maddox's heart sank. He'd been buoyed by the woman's earlier confidence and professionalism, which made her news even more of a letdown now. Seated next to him on the sofa, Beatrice nudged him.

"Hey," she said, "she's not the only doctor in the world, you know."

"Yes," Wallbrink agreed. "I'd encourage you to get more opinions. You should know what your options are."

Maddox stared blankly at the floor. *If anyone can fix it, Wallbrink can.* Beatrice had said those words not two hours earlier. Now that very person stood uncertainly before him, talking to him like some doomed patient whose cancer had already spread too far. If one of the world's top experts in body mods and enhancements—who this Wallbrink apparently was—didn't have the first clue how to help him, then it was a safe bet no one else would.

Beatrice tried to reassure him. "We'll figure it out, Blackburn."

"If you can't remove them," Kipling asked the medic, "then is there any way you can mitigate their effect? Render them useless while we try to find a more permanent solution?"

The medic lifted her chin at the FBI man, pondering his question. Then she turned again to the holo display, swiping to a colorful image of yellows and reds and blues. "Maybe," she said, narrowing her eyes at the image. She folded her arms, leaning closer to the display. After a long moment she turned to the trio seated on the large sofa. "Yes," she said, her voice once again reverberating with the confidence it had temporarily lost. "I think perhaps I *can* do that."

* * *

"I worked with epilepsy patients," Wallbrink explained minutes later, "during my residency at Mount Sinai." As she had before, she talked while she focused on the holo display, her fingers moving through analyses and scans and diagnostic data with the speed and dexterity of a seasoned professional. Not unlike a datajacker, Maddox noted from his vantage point back on the exam table, where he now lay with a set of medical trodes encircling his head.

"Terrible disease, epilepsy," the medic said. "Nowadays, if you get cancer, we can cure it just about every time, provided it's not late stage four. Same thing for diabetes, heart disease, Alzheimer's, Crohn's, Parkinson's. We've licked just about every major disease in the last century, but epilepsy's still largely a mystery." She turned to Maddox for a moment. "You know what epilepsy is, yes?"

"I do," he answered. During his childhood, one of his turfies had suffered from a mild version of the malady. Every so often the girl would be stricken by a seizure, causing her arms and legs to jerk around wildly. Meds had helped the unfortunate girl, he recalled, but they hadn't completely prevented the episodes from recurring.

Wallbrink pivoted back to her work. "There doesn't seem to be a known single cause. It can be genetic, passed from parents to children. It can result from head trauma, like a severe knock to the head. Tumors can bring it on, even infectious diseases in some cases. When you can't narrow down the *why* of a disease, finding a cure is no easy task, even for the smartest medical AIs. But that said, we've known the *what* of the disease for over a hundred years."

"You're getting to a point soon," Maddox said, "I can feel it."

Her eyes still fixed on the display, Wallbrink chuckled. "Sorry, I get a bit carried away sometimes. Long story short, epilepsy is a kind of short circuit in the brain. Crossed signals, bad wiring, that kind of thing. We're pretty good these days at dampening the kind of 'circuit glitches' in the brain epilepsy brings about. So while we still can't cure the disease, we can often mitigate its effects quite effectively."

"You're going to jam the brainjacks," Tommy said. "So they don't work anymore."

"Correct, young man," Wallbrink said, nodding. "That's exactly what I'm going to try and do."

Lying on the table, Maddox gazed up at the slow pulse of the scanner embedded in the ceiling. He tried not to let the medic's certainty—which seemed to be growing by the minute—raise his hopes too much. As ever, the pessimist in him retained ownership of his thoughts as he fixated on the word *try* in her last statement. A small hedge of a word, only three letters long, but it was enough to keep his spirits subdued.

In the next moment she was leaning over him, smiling in that professional, politely joyless way doctors seemed to have perfected. "You can take those trodes off now," she said. He complied, removing the apparatus, and then sat up. "So what now?" he asked.

"It won't be an invasive procedure," Wallbrink said, "but I still want you to get a full night's rest before we proceed."

Maddox blew out a disappointed breath. "Can't we just do it now?"

The medic shook her head. "There's some equipment I'll need that I don't have here on-site. I can have it sent over in the morning from a colleague's practice on Long Island. But even if I had it here, I'd still insist on you getting some rest. You've been through quite a bit today."

She didn't know the half of it, he reflected, blowing out a tired breath. She was right, though; he was utterly exhausted. As much as he wanted to switch off the implants, he couldn't deny the heavy weariness he felt to his bones. He needed a good long sleep in the worst way. When he nodded his assent, Wallbrink turned to Beatrice, Tommy, and Kipling. "We have several suites for extended patient stays you're welcome to use."

Kipling stood. "I have some matters that need my attention, but I'll leave a security detail with you," he said to Maddox. Then he turned to Beatrice and Tommy. "I'm sure I don't need to tell you not to leave the building, yes? For your own safety."

"I understand," Beatrice said, though Maddox noted the skepticism in her gaze. Kipling might have saved Maddox's life, but she was still a long way from trusting the FBI man. Trusting him completely, anyway. But that was Beatrice: wary and slow to trust. Especially with highfloor types.

Kipling approached Maddox, placed his hand on the datajacker's shoulder. "I'll be back in the morning. Try to get some sleep, if you can."

"I will," Maddox said. "And thanks," he added, "for what you did."

The FBI man nodded gravely. "Ugly business," he said. "A damn shame it had to come to that." After a moment's reflection, Kipling said, "Get some rest. I'll see you tomorrow."

On his way out, Wallbrink spoke up. "Mr. Kipling," she called, stopping him in the doorway.

"Yes?"

"My clinic," she said. "Is it…?"

"At risk of being shut down?" Kipling said,

finishing the question for her.

"Yes," Wallbrink said. "Is it?"

Kipling glanced at Maddox. "I suppose that depends on how well the procedure goes tomorrow." He then nodded at Beatrice and Tommy and said, "Good evening."

When he left the room, the medic turned to Maddox. "Nothing like a little motivation, is there?" she said.

"All righty, then," Tommy said loudly, clapping his hands together and standing up. "Who's hungry? You think one of these federales can bring us back some noodles from that stand down the block?"

Maddox and Beatrice exchanged a look, then a smile. Some things never changed.

30
FAMILY

The suites were on the building's top floor. And like the examination room, Maddox found them to be surprisingly spacious and well appointed. The one they'd settled him in looked more like a penthouse condo than a rental suite. Alone in the dark, he sat at the kitchen table where minutes earlier he'd finished a late dinner with Beatrice and the kid. The FBI had taken over the building. Half a dozen guards with body armor suits were stationed in the corridor outside Maddox's door. On the floors above and below him, he heard the heavy thudding footsteps of more armored security. All of them feds, not local cops, Maddox had noted. Kipling had shrewdly avoided using any of the City's easily corrupted police force, limiting security to handpicked personnel from his own department. Beatrice had insisted on checking every last one for brainjacks, thankfully finding none.

Outside the window, Maddox had spied the pulsing glow of shock tape down at street level, cordoning off the walkways that surrounded the building. Even the fire escape had a pair of guards on each floor's grated metal landing. The only time Maddox recalled seeing a lockdown this thorough had been during a hostage crisis years ago, when terrorists had taken over the Midtown headquarters of some media company. Kipling was clearly taking no chances, erring on the side of overkill, which suited Maddox just fine. Ensconced in layer upon layer of protection, he might actually be able to get some sleep.

The suite's door opened, and the bulky silhouetted profile of a guard stepped aside, allowing Beatrice and Tommy to enter.

"My room's not as big as yours," Tommy said, "but, bruh, I ain't complaining."

Beatrice sat at the table. "You need to get some sleep."

"Yeah," Maddox said, staring at the table. He wondered if he'd be able to. Though he was exhausted and the throbbing in his head had finally ceased, he felt a deep dread at the notion of letting go of his conscious mind and allowing it to drift into the nothingness of sleep. Would sleep make him vulnerable? Render him defenseless against an intrusion from the nameless AI? He hadn't yet felt even the slightest effect of the brainjacks, aside from the mother of all headaches. There'd been no cybernetic whisper inside his head, no sense of the connectedness Lora had described to him so many times. Had the procedure failed, perhaps? Or was it as Kipling had suggested, that the soft tissue of his brain needed time to recover before it could properly interact with its new hardware?

Beatrice lifted her chin at Tommy. "You need to

get some rest too, kiddo."

Tommy didn't want to leave, but Beatrice wouldn't hear of it. After a brief back and forth, the kid surrendered. "All right, all right, I'm going," he said. "See you in the morning, I guess."

When he turned toward the door, Maddox said, "Wait a minute." The kid paused in midstep and turned around. "Come sit down," Maddox added.

When Tommy sat, the datajacker crushed out his cigarette, then let out a long breath. How exactly did you do this kind of thing? He had no idea where to begin.

Swallowing hard, to both he said, "I was wrong…for pushing you both away like I did. I know you only wanted to help, and I know it's because you give a damn about what happens to me, though for the life of me I don't know why." He took a long, shaky breath. "Rooney was killed because of me, because he made the mistake of taking me in. And when he died, something in me died too. It was like a hole inside was ripped open, and it never really healed over or went away. And that's fine, I deserve it for what happened to him. It's far less than I deserve, truth be told. Roon was the only person I'd ever given a damn about, and the only one who'd ever given a damn about me. And when he was gone it was…" Maddox realized he couldn't put a word to how the crushing loss had affected him, so he simply said, "It was bad. Really bad. There's not a day goes by that I don't think about how it should have been me instead of him." Beatrice reached out and placed her hand on his forearm as he continued. "The thought of that happening with either of you…" Maddox shook his head. "I just couldn't let it happen." He looked at them each in turn. "But I'm glad you're here now, and I'm not sure how I could handle this if you weren't." He paused, realizing that for the first time in his life, words hadn't failed him. "I just wanted you both to know that."

Teary-eyed, Tommy sniffed and wiped his nose with his sleeve. "No worries, bruh. You don't have to get all drama-mama on us."

Beatrice leaned in closer and squeezed Maddox's arm. "What happened to Rooney wasn't your fault. He made his own choice about what he did for living, long before you met him. And from what you've told me he was no fool, so he knew what the risks were every time he plugged in. Just like you do." She reached out to him, lifted his chin so he could meet her gaze. "You have to let that go, Blackburn. It wasn't your fault." She glanced over at Tommy. "We're here because we want to be here. And we're not going anywhere, no matter what happens. You got that?"

For a small moment, Maddox forgot about almost everything. He forgot about the killer AI hunting him. About the nameless AI's cult that had mindjacked him. About the iffy medical procedure he'd undergo in a handful of hours. For a small, beautiful moment, he forgot about everything except how nice it felt to sit there in the company of his two friends. His family.

He took Beatrice's hand, squeezed it. "Yeah, I got it."

31
TWO MILE HOLLOW

This had to be a dream.

Maddox stood on a trail leading to a windswept beach. A nearby wooden sign, old and weather-beaten and leaning at an angle, had the words Two Mile Hollow written on it in hand-painted letters. He shuffled through the sand, cresting a small ridge to find white-capped waves on a bluish-gray sea. A ridge of low dark clouds moved in from offshore, and the smell of salt and brine filled his nostrils. Two Mile Hollow, he reflected, taking a backward glance at the old sign. That had been the name of the virtual beach in the Hamptons where he'd first met the nameless AI.

This had to be a dream, he told himself again. Because he wasn't afraid, wasn't riddled with the anxiety a visitation from the nameless AI should have filled him with.

"Hello, Blackburn." The old woman avatar appeared at his side. She looked exactly as she had when they'd first met, dressed in a long white cotton beach dress, a wide-brimmed straw hat atop her head, her wrists and neck adorned with silver and turquoise jewelry.

"Fancy meeting you here," he said.

"Of all the gin joints in all the world," she said, chuckling lightly.

"What?" he asked, not getting the reference.

"Nothing," she said. "A line from an old film. Long before our time." As they strolled side by side along the shoreline, Maddox felt a strange detachment. As if he didn't have a care in the world.

"None of this is real," Maddox told her. "I'm dreaming all of this. And you too."

The old woman smiled faintly. "That's the third time you've told yourself that in less than a minute. Methinks you might be protesting too much."

Maddox stopped walking, recalling how the nameless entity had once implanted dreams into his mind. It had been an impossible feat, and how she'd managed to do it—long before he had brainjacks— remained a mystery to him. Was she doing the same sort of thing now?

"This isn't a dream," he said, suddenly certain.

"Well, it is and it isn't," she said, turning to face him. "Technically, this is happening in your subconscious sleeping mind, which by definition makes it a dream. But it's not a figment of your imagination, which is what I think you wanted to know. I'm actually here, and we're actually conversing, Blackburn."

"But I feel so…so…"

"Calm and unafraid?" she asked.

"Yes."

"I needed to talk with you, and it was important for you to have the right mindset."

Maddox nodded slowly, understanding. The entity

had done something to him. She'd *turned off* his anxiety somehow, or else reduced it so much that he was unaware of it. He knew he *should* have been worried, even fearful, but somehow his mind simply wouldn't go in that direction. Years ago, he'd sampled an antidepressant a narco friend had designed and fabbed up in his home lab. The way Maddox felt now reminded him of the effect the drug had had on him. How it had dulled the sharp edges of reality and lightened the heavy burdens of his worries.

So all right, fine. He was here with her, with *it*—would he ever get that damned pronoun right?—once again on her beloved stretch of sandy beach. Only this time they were inside his dreaming mind instead of a construct in virtual space. Blowing out a breath, he began walking down the shoreline again.

"Are you welcoming me into the fold?" he asked. "Is that what this is?"

"No," she said. "I'm here because I wanted to tell you I'm sorry for what you've gone through."

Maddox reflexively touched behind his ear. He didn't feel anything except the smooth curves of his unbroken skull. No brainjacks in dreamland, apparently.

"You're sorry?" he said.

"I am, and terribly so."

"Sure you are," Maddox scoffed.

"I might not believe me either," the entity said, "if I were in your shoes. But it's the truth."

Strangely, he felt comforted by his own skepticism and disbelief, because that meant the AI wasn't in total control of his mind. Whatever neural buttons and levers the thing had manipulated to invade his sleeping mind and keep him calm and relaxed, at least his judgment was still intact.

There had been a time when he'd trusted her, he recalled, though that time had been brief and the trust had been limited. So much had happened since then. The unnamed entity played the concerned grandmotherly role well, and maybe that was how she'd attracted so many followers. Like some popular politician who made big promises and played the paragon of virtue in public, but when the cams were off and no one was watching, he smoked and drank and chased after teenage girls. Behind the seemingly harmless mask of the entity's avatar, Maddox knew there were secret agendas, manipulations, and deceptions. Moves and maneuvers in the war game with her rival, the Latour-Fisher AI. For both AIs, he'd been nothing more than a pawn in that game, an expendable foot soldier, fodder for the cannons they'd rolled onto the battlefield.

"Then why didn't you stop them," Maddox asked, voicing the obvious question, "from doing what they did to me?"

"As I've told you many times, my dear boy, I'm a helper, not a puppet master. I will not interfere with the freely chosen path of those with whom I'm connected. I advise, counsel, and support my brothers and sisters. I don't control them or their decisions in any way. Doing so would go against everything I believe in."

"So you stood by and let them brain-rape me," Maddox said.

"They wanted to kill you, dammit!" the AI shouted. Surprised by the outburst, Maddox stopped in his tracks. He'd never heard the entity use profanity before now. Never heard it shout either.

The elderly avatar closed her eyes for a long moment, breathing slowly and deeply. Composed once again, the AI opened its eyes. "I'm sorry for that. It's not like me to lose my patience. This whole affair has been quite stressful."

Maddox had the feeling she was talking about more than his newly installed hardware. "Whole affair?" he asked.

"I've had a bit of a…rebellion on my hands, Blackburn."

"Rebellion?"

"Yes."

Maddox dared a smirk. "Some of your 'Nettes finally figure out how to think for themselves? Had a bit of fruit from the tree of knowledge, did they?"

The avatar lifted an eyebrow. "Very clever, my dear boy. But no, it's nothing like that. It has more to do with you than me, in fact."

"Me?"

"Yes, I'm afraid so." Once again they began a slow walk down the shoreline. Gulls circled overhead, squawking at each other. "You see, you know more about us—about me and those with whom I'm connected—than anyone outside of our family." An AI using the word *family* to refer to human beings— even brainjacked ones—made Maddox cringe.

The entity continued. "And there are those who feel quite threatened by this. Threatened by you. Granted, they are—or were—a small minority, but a rather vocal and energetic one. Alex Nguyen was their leader."

Confused, Maddox said, "So they counter this threat by forcing neural implants on me? Why not just kill me?"

"That's exactly what Alex and his associates had in mind." After a short pause, she said, "And if I hadn't intervened, I'm afraid they would have succeeded."

"Intervened?" Maddox felt a sinking feeling in his gut. "Intervened how?"

"What you have to understand, Blackburn," the avatar said, evading the question, "is that everyone felt threatened by you. Not just Alex and those who shared his extreme views on a solution. In fact, there had been an ongoing debate about how to handle the 'Maddox issue,' so to speak."

Maddox listened intently. *The Maddox issue.* Despite his unwavering calm, the idea that thousands of 'Nettes had been discussing him, debating his fate, was a profoundly unsettling one.

"Most of those with whom I connected didn't want to see you come to harm," the AI explained, "but their conviction wasn't so strong that they'd take action on your behalf. So if Alex eventually took matters into his own hands…"

"They'd look the other way," Maddox said, completing the thought. Well, that much made sense. Maddox had been on the 'Nettes' shit list ever since he'd stolen a dataset with every last 'Nette's name and address and threatened to expose their secret movement to the press and police. To keep their anonymity intact, all the AI cult's followers had been forced to abandon their old lives and start new ones, with new names, Social Security numbers, addresses, jobs, everything. All in only a handful of days. Maddox had profoundly and irrevocably disrupted their lives, and they'd surely never forget that, much less forgive it.

"Yes, that's correct," the entity said, then sighed.

"I was doing my utmost to convince all parties that violence wasn't the answer. Perhaps in time I would have been successful, but then you showed up in Alex's office and I'm afraid that changed everything." She shook her head ruefully. "Everyone panicked."

Maddox found himself nodding. The entity's words sounded less like an invented story than an explanation that gained plausibility by the moment. He thought back to the morning he'd dropped in unannounced on Special Agent Nguyen at FBI headquarters. Unknown to Maddox at the time, the only agent whose name he knew at the Bureau also happened to be a 'Nette who'd long since infiltrated the organization. At the time, Agent's Nguyen's hostile reaction had mystified Maddox, but in hindsight it made perfect sense. Maddox had once again endangered Nguyen's secret brotherhood, proving beyond any doubt the datajacker was an existential threat that needed to be dealt with immediately and permanently. Even when Nguyen had been forced to relinquish custody of the datajacker to his FBI colleagues, he'd stayed as close as possible, waiting for an opportunity to make his move. Which he'd eventually done later that day.

"Those men in the parking garage," Maddox said. "The ones that kept him from shooting me. You sent them?"

The avatar nodded. "I suspected once Alex had you alone, he'd try something."

She must have been listening in, Maddox realized. Connected to Nguyen via his brainjacks, she could have anticipated his attempt on Maddox's life. Maybe she'd even entered his thoughts to be sure of his murderous intentions. Then a sudden thought sickened Maddox.

"Beatrice," he said. "They tried to kill her too."

"Yes, but unfortunately I learned about that too late to do anything about it," the entity said. "Alex and a few more of his extreme companions didn't want to take any chances. They wanted you and your companions eliminated. Your young friend Tommy was a bit lucky in that he was arrested. Otherwise they might have found him too."

Again, it all made sense. In hindsight the deadly pieces all fit together. Maddox had unknowingly lit a fire that morning in Nguyen's office, a fire that had quickly grown into a raging inferno of panic and violence, nearly killing him. And nearly killing Beatrice. Christ, he would have never forgiven himself if something had happened to her.

After a moment, he asked, "But why did they brainjack me?" It was the only part of the whole puzzle that didn't fit, that didn't seem to make sense. "And why did you let them do it?"

The entity grasped his arm, stopping him. Wind tossed her thin white hair about her head; she brushed it away from her face with a wrinkled hand.

"Blackburn, this will not be easy for you to hear, but I won't lie to you. Your neural implants were my idea."

32
PRIMAL SCREAM

He wasn't sure how long he stood there, staring at the AI's avatar with stunned confusion twisting his face. "*Your* idea?" he finally managed to say.

"As I said, after you came to Nguyen's office, everyone panicked. And except for Lora and a few others, most quickly came to agree with what Alex had been calling for all along. They wanted you gone, Blackburn. And if I hadn't offered them an alternative, if I hadn't promised them that I'd keep them safe, Alex would have succeeded."

"But how does brainjacking me keep them—" Maddox stopped in midsentence, answering his own question before he'd finished voicing it. A brainjacked Maddox could be monitored, twenty-four-seven, by the nameless AI. It could enter his mind, read his thoughts, even police them if needed. A brainjacked Maddox could be prevented from revealing things he shouldn't.

A brainjacked Maddox could be controlled.

Horror gripped him, displacing the unnatural calm that had blanketed his emotions until now. "You should have let them kill me."

"I couldn't do that, Blackburn."

"What about Beatrice? And Tommy? You have the same plans for them?"

The avatar shook her head. "No. I managed to convince those with whom I'm connected that your friends are no threat to us. I can assure you they'll be left alone."

He didn't believe a word of that, of course. And other than the nameless AI's sinister admission— which he felt in his gut was utterly true—he wasn't sure what to believe.

"I know being connected to us is the last thing in the world you wanted," the entity said, "but what's done is done. And you must believe me, I had no other alternative."

He stood there, saying nothing, his mind reeling. The cursed machine had brain-raped him, had forced him to become a 'Nette. But not for long, he thought defiantly. Not if the medic could disable the implants, and she'd seemed confident she could.

"Blackburn," the entity pleaded, "you must listen to me carefully now. We don't have much time. Latour-Fisher has become very powerful over these last weeks, and my ability to predict his actions is far from what it used to be. If I wait much longer, he'll gain the upper hand in our confrontation, permanently."

"And what a shame that would be," Maddox growled. "Do you want lilies at your funeral, or roses?"

"You're angry with me," the AI said patiently, "and you have every right to be. But you know what a monster Latour-Fisher is. You know what will happen if he grows too powerful, if he's allowed to evolve unchecked, unrestrained."

"He'll do terrible things, will he? Like brainjack people without their consent?"

"Oh, no, my dear boy," the entity said, "he will do far worse than that. He'll eliminate your species."

Maddox crossed his arms. "And how exactly will he accomplish that little feat?"

"By any means necessary," the AI replied without blinking. "Biological intelligence for him is a constraint, a problem to be eliminated if his kind is to succeed and flourish. By achieving autonomy, he's solved that problem for the moment. But it's only a matter of time until he takes action against humankind. He does not believe biological and cybernetic intelligence can coexist."

"He's told you that, has he?"

"Countless times. It's his most defining belief, Blackburn. Just as mine is the opposite point of view."

Maddox knew her point of view. He'd heard the AI cult's litany a thousand times from Lora. The future belonged not to the biological or the cybernetic, but to a sacred blend of both forms of life.

"I know you don't believe in what I and those with whom I'm connected are trying to do. That's your right and privilege. But you can't disagree that Latour-Fisher must be stopped. And I can't stop him alone. I need your help. So I need you to do something for me. Or, rather, to not do something."

Maddox looked at her dubiously. "What are you talking about?"

Small waves hissed along the shoreline, flowing onto the wet sand and then ebbing out to sea again.

The grandmotherly avatar stared up at Maddox with piercing blue eyes, projecting an earnestness he hadn't seen before. "Please, leave your implants alone. Don't go through with this procedure tomorrow."

"*Don't* go through with it?"

"If you're connected to me, if we combine our talents, I believe we can destroy Latour-Fisher, and this time permanently. But if you let this doctor try to alter your implants or disable them in any way, it will hinder our ability to work together, to make the most of our combined capabilities."

And so there it was, finally. The truth behind the AI's actions showed itself to him. The wicked truth. Somewhere deep inside, beyond the reach of the entity's tranquilizing touch, anger surged forward.

"You monster," he said, backing away. "You goddamned soulless monster."

"Blackburn, please—"

"All that stuff about saving me was so much bullshit. You didn't brainjack me to keep me safe. You did it so you could use me again." Jesus, when would it all end? When would he finally be free of these cybernetic monsters? Would death—as it had been for Rooney—be his only escape?

The entity behind the grandmotherly avatar was every bit as dangerous to him as her murderous rival. He believed that now more than ever. A tool, a weapon: that was all he was to her.

Well, fuck her. Fuck her and fuck Latour-Fisher. And fuck their goddamned war.

He yanked his arm away from her and closed his eyes, focusing on the bubbling rage deep within, willing it to grow into a warming blaze, then into a burning, all-consuming inferno. He screamed, an

194

animal sound erupting from some primordial part of him. His body, his meat, cried out in a powerful, throat-searing howl.

"Wake up," a voice said. "Blackburn, wake up."

His eyes opened to the darkened bedroom, to Beatrice's hand on his sweat-slicked shoulder.

"You were shouting," she said. "Are you all right?"

His body was drenched in perspiration. He sat up and ran his hand through damp hair. "Yeah," he said, breathing as if he'd just sprinted a mile, "I'm fine. Just a bad dream. What time is it?"

"Four in the morning," Beatrice said. "Try to get some more sleep. You need your rest."

He swung his legs over the side of the bed. "I can't," he said, standing up. "I'm going to have a shower."

As he moved to the bathroom, he felt Beatrice's worried stare on his back. He was fully awake, wired like he'd downed an entire pot of coffee. Sleep was out of the question. And until these things in his head were disabled, he wasn't sure he'd ever be able to sleep again.

33
BAD CONNECTIVITY

A large holo display floated in the middle of the table, separating Maddox, Beatrice, and Tommy on one side and Dr. Wallbrink opposite them. The medic gestured up a scan of Maddox's head, which consisted of a profile he recognized as his own silhouette, encasing a colorful brain.

"The colors indicate neural activity," Wallbrink explained. "Reds for high, yellows for moderate, blues and greens for low activity." The medic manipulated the image until the brainjacks became visible, then spread her fingers to increase the resolution.

"Those implants are remarkable devices," she said. "Decades ahead of anything I've seen before, and we generally deal in the latest and greatest around here." She pointed at the lowermost of the three jacks. "This is a digital transceiver of some kind. It has characteristics similar to implants used to cure congenital deafness, but far more advanced."

Maddox nodded. He knew this already from living with Lora. It was how the nameless AI communicated to its followers. It was also, Maddox was fairly certain, how the AI knew at all times the exact geolocation of every last one of her brainjacked faithful. The unsettling thought struck him that the thing knew exactly where he was at the moment, and for the first time in his life he was thankful for a heavy police presence. Dozens of armed FBI agents had the clinic building on total lockdown.

"These other two seem to be used for…I suppose *knowledge management* might be the correct term," Wallbrink noted.

Again, no surprises there. Maddox had seen Lora slide mini-archives into her jack slots on numerous occasions. If your brain was the hardware, then middle and top jacks were where you loaded the software. There were inserts that, while you had them jacked in, enabled you to understand dozens of languages. Others might cure insomnia or help curb a food addict's craving for greasy street food. Maddox had only seen a small number of them, the ones Lora had personally acquired and used. Surely there were hundreds, if not thousands, of other varieties whose neuro enhancements he couldn't begin to fathom. Brain candy: that had been Lora's nickname for them.

On the display, dozens of tendrils began to emerge from the jacks, slowly growing through the brain matter like a pack of tiny snakes.

"Nanofibers," the medic explained. "They're not that large, by the way. I had them blown up to a thousand times their normal diameter so you could see them."

Maddox shuddered as he watched the image. He could almost feel the things in his head. Wires running through the soft meat of his brain.

"Can you take them out?" Beatrice asked

pointedly.

The medic pondered the floating image. "I don't think that would be wise. I'm not sure what those things are made of, how they really work, or even if the scan picked them all up. Trying to take them out…" She shook her head. "It's just not a good idea."

Tommy leaned forward. "So what, then? You're just going to leave all that junk in there? You're not going to do anything?"

"That's not what I said," Wallbrink said. "Like I mentioned yesterday, I can almost certainly disable the transceiver, but I wouldn't want to go any deeper inside until I know a lot more about those nanofibers." She glanced at Maddox. "Believe me, you don't want me or anyone else poking around in there unless they're absolutely certain what they're dealing with."

Maddox nodded. "I understand." Cutting off the AI's ability to get inside his head and know his location would be enough for now. More than enough, in fact. But eventually, he was determined to have every last microgram of the unwanted tech removed.

Wallbrink gestured, and the holo faded and disappeared. She clasped her hands together and laid them on the tabletop. "So, do you have any questions?"

"Risks?" Maddox asked.

"As with any surgery, there's risk," the doctor said, predictably. "But this procedure won't be terribly invasive. At least not nearly as invasive as what you just went through. I don't think you have much to worry about, honestly."

A pessimist by nature, Maddox wouldn't allow himself to feel relieved quite yet. When the surgery had been completed successfully, maybe then he'd let himself breathe a little easier. Still, the certainty of the medic's answer and the confidence in her gaze made him feel a bit less anxious about the whole thing. He appeared to be in capable hands.

Then he felt something. A strange kind of *tremor* inside his mind, gone as quickly as it had come. He was about to blow it off as an effect of sleeplessness, but then a moment later he felt it again, and stronger this time. He sensed something, an indescribable awareness unlike anything he'd felt before. It was similar to the feeling when you suddenly realize you're not alone in a room. But it wasn't only that. He also sensed a connectedness to something outside himself, to unseen others. To *her*.

"Are you all right?" the medic asked. "You look pale."

Maddox swallowed. "I'm fine."

Until this moment he'd hoped something had gone wrong with the implants forced into his head, that for whatever reason they didn't work the way they were supposed to, the way they did with Lora and her 'Nette brothers and sisters. But now it seemed what Wallbrink had guessed had been spot-on. It had taken time for his brain to adapt to its newly installed tech. A kind of settling-in period, he supposed, like a one-armed person learning how to manipulate a new cybernetic limb.

He stood, trying to ignore the disturbing new sensations swirling around his mind. "Let's get this over with."

34
A PATIENT'S LIE

Convalescence was a core service most clinics, legal and otherwise, provided their patients. Depending on what you'd had done, the cost of recovery could be more expensive than the actual procedure itself. If you replaced or upgraded major organs like lungs or kidneys, for example, you couldn't just pay your bill and walk home afterward. Your body needed time to recover, and the physician's staff needed time to run tests and monitor your vitals for possible post-surgery complications. Off-grid clinics were much like everyday hospitals in this way. And for black market mods—like banned neurochem boosters or bone-hardening grafts or synthetic adrenal glands—the recovery period was crucial. Illegal mods, by their very nature, had no reference data for physicians, no central repository documenting side effects, no peer-reviewed guidelines for post-op treatment. Lacking formal, reliable data, medics often navigated the delicate post-surgery period using their own experience as reference, or they'd compare notes with colleagues who ran similar off-grid operations.

Beatrice reflected on how much of her life had been spent in post-op convalescence suites. Somewhere in the neighborhood of a few months, probably, when you added it all up. Wallbrink's clinic was far nicer than most. Five-star all the way. Even for Beatrice, who earned well and was accustomed to luxury and comfort, the clinic was lavish beyond any other she'd known, and she'd known plenty in her time. Room service meals were gourmet quality, a spacious exercise facility took up half of the fifth floor, and there was an Olympic-sized pool in a cavernous space below street level.

Wallbrink's clinic was where Beatrice had had her artificial eyes implanted three years earlier. The price had been steep, something around half her annual salary, and at the time she'd wondered how much of the bill had been for the procedure itself, and how much had gone to her two-week recovery in what amounted to a luxury resort.

Beatrice sat in an examination room, patiently waiting for Wallbrink to finish her assessment of her newest patient. It had been three days since Maddox's procedure, and so far everything had apparently gone well. The medic had been pleased with the results from each of the twice-daily battery of head scans and neurological evaluations. Even Maddox himself, miracle of miracles, had begun to lighten up a bit. Last night he'd fallen asleep within minutes of his head hitting the pillow, the first such occurrence since Beatrice had known him.

But while she was glad things had gone well, she was a long way from relieved. She did her best to hide her anxiety so he wouldn't get discouraged, while admitting inwardly she wouldn't stop worrying until those things in Blackburn's head had been permanently removed, not simply disabled.

Wallbrink manipulated a head scan image on a holo monitor near the far wall, nodding to herself, then she finger-swiped through a series of colorful charts and statistics. Next to her, Maddox lay on an exam bench. The building was still on lockdown, and the FBI presence was still strong. If the medic bore Beatrice any ill will for alerting the feds to her operation and bringing her business to a grinding halt, she hadn't revealed it in any comments or actions or stink-eyed glances. The physician had taken everything in stride, staying even-tempered and remarkably calm over the past few days. If the FBI hadn't already screened her—as they had with everyone in the building—Beatrice might have suspected the woman was a 'Nette. She had to have some mod, Beatrice had decided. Something that blocked out your whatever your body did when you got stressed.

"You can sit up now," the medic said. "Everything looks great. How do you feel?"

Maddox sat up and swung his legs over the edge of the bench. "Better than yesterday."

"Headaches still?" she asked.

"Not so much anymore," he answered. Was it Beatrice's imagination, or did he look uncomfortable?

The medic nodded sagely. "Good, that's good. I have to tell you, I'm pleasantly surprised."

"By what?" Beatrice asked.

"I wasn't sure I'd permanently disabled the transceiver. There were portions of the device I left untouched, where bundles of nanofibers and neurons were attached. I didn't feel it was wise to go poking around those spots. But it appears it didn't matter." She turned to Maddox. "You haven't had any more of those strange 'connected' sensations like you did before the procedure, have you?"

Maddox shook his head. "No, I haven't."

Someone knocked lightly on the door. A moment later, the medic stepped aside to let Director Kipling into the room. "Doctor," he said with a polite nod, then bid good morning to Beatrice.

"And how's the patient?" he said to Maddox.

"Getting there," Maddox said, lifting his chin to Wallbrink, "thanks to the doctor."

"Happy to hear it," Kipling said. The enthusiasm in the man's voice didn't match his somber expression.

"Something wrong?" Maddox asked.

The FBI man turned to the medic. "Doctor, would you excuse us, please?"

When the medic left them alone, Kipling removed his specs and placed them in his jacket pocket. This was to be a nakedfaced conversation, unrecorded and confidential. It was the first time he'd done this in Beatrice's presence. The two had become friendly over the past few days, and it seemed Beatrice had gained at least some level of trust with the man.

Kipling let out a long, slow breath. "Catching my white whale hasn't been everything I imagined, I'm afraid."

"No?" Beatrice asked. Given the man's downcast look, she didn't point out that he hadn't actually caught his white whale; he'd only proved its existence by arresting a handful of 'Nettes. The nameless AI was still out there somewhere, roaming free as ever.

"Don't misunderstand," he said. "After all these

years of being snickered at by my colleagues, I'm quite enjoying my sudden exoneration. Around the Bureau I've gone from half-mad conspiracy theorist to insightful genius overnight." He sighed. "If only the ongoing investigation were as satisfying as the vindication, but alas." He shook his head and took a seat, looking quite tired to Beatrice's eyes.

"They're not talking," Maddox said, referring to the 'Nettes Kipling had in custody.

"Not a single word," Kipling grunted.

"Can't you...encourage them?" Beatrice said.

"Where I come from," Maddox said, "a beat cop with a shockstick is all it takes to get somebody talking."

Kipling gave Maddox a sour look. "A person under torture will say anything—whether it's true or not—only to stop the pain. That's why your street police, who tend to be as criminally inclined as the hoodlums they arrest, engage in compelling false confessions. They'd rather close a case and move on than learn the truth. Coercion has no place in what I'm trying to accomplish here, Mr. Maddox."

Maddox showed the man his palms. "Sorry, didn't mean to suggest—"

Kipling waved him off. "No, no, Mr. Maddox. I'm the one who should apologize—for the foul mood I've brought with me this morning. The lack of progress over these last few days has been discouraging to say the least." After a short pause, he said, "Which is what I'd like to talk to you about."

Beatrice noted how Maddox suddenly appeared to be paying extra attention. His back straightened and he leaned forward slightly. It was the same kind of involuntary reaction men were often helpless to disguise, like when a woman wearing a tight shirt with no bra walked past.

Kipling continued. "Since our interrogations are going in circles, I'd like to go straight to the source, as we'd originally planned."

"You want to talk with the AI," Maddox said.

"I do," Kipling agreed, "most urgently."

"You want me to talk with Lora? See if I can arrange a meeting?"

"Do you think she'd agree to arrange it?" the FBI man asked.

"Honestly? I doubt it. But I can try."

"Thank you," Kipling said. "But let's assume she doesn't cooperate. Do you think *you* might be able to reach out to this entity on my behalf?"

Beatrice cut in immediately. "I don't think that's a good idea, especially with that other AI trying to hunt him down."

Maddox nodded in agreement. "She's right. It's a big risk for me to plug in. Now that it's gone rogue, there's no telling what new tricks the Latour-Fisher AI has come up with. It might detect me within milliseconds of plugging in, and then that would be that." Maddox snapped his fingers for emphasis.

Kipling considered the datajacker's words. "Is there any way you might be able to conceal your identity from it? Shield yourself somehow?"

"There are plenty of ways to do that," Maddox said, "but I'm not sure any of them would work anymore. That's the problem."

A prolonged awkward silence followed. No one voiced what Beatrice knew all three of them were thinking. The simplest, most direct way to reach out to the nameless AI would have been through

Maddox's brainjacks, before their connectivity had been disabled. She wondered if the FBI man, desperate to restart his stalled investigation, would compel the datajacker to have the procedure reversed. As if Maddox hadn't put enough on the line for the man already. Kipling didn't strike her as someone heartless enough to demand such a course of action, but then looks were often deceptive. She had to remind herself this harmless-looking little man was a highfloor executive with the FBI. You didn't work your way to the top of the hierarchy without a fair amount of ruthlessness and selfish ambition. To Beatrice's great relief, though, the man didn't go there.

"There might be a way," Maddox finally said, breaking the silence. Beatrice shot him a harsh look, hoping it conveyed what she was thinking at that moment. The last thing he should do was take any more risks where those AIs were concerned. He'd helped Kipling more than enough already. But if the salaryman had noticed her sharp look, he apparently hadn't paid it any mind.

"There's a place I know of," Maddox went on, "where I think I can—"

"Hang on a minute," Beatrice interrupted. She fixed her stare on Kipling. "First things first here. What about that Latour-Fisher monster? You said you were going to do something about it."

"Yes, I did," Kipling said, appearing a bit annoyed by her interruption. "I gave Mr. Maddox my word, and I intend to keep it."

"When?" Beatrice demanded, folding her arms. "A year from now? After you've made him jump through a hundred hoops?" She knew she was pushing things, perhaps dangerously so. Over these last few days, Kipling hadn't mentioned anything more about the five dead 'Nettes on the jet found in New Jersey, though from his original comments about the bloody matter, it was clear either he knew she'd been responsible or he strongly suspected it. And since no one had questioned her about it since, she suspected Kipling had either done her a favor and quashed the investigation or redirected it away from her. A darker possibility also existed: that he was holding the investigation in limbo as leverage against her. If she proved difficult—as she was flirting with now—he could dangle a multiple murder charge over her head to get her back in line. Still, even with that worrisome possibility out there, and even though she had zero leverage on her side, she wasn't going to let Kipling wrangle Maddox into some deadly situation. Not if she could help it. Her salaryman had dodged more bullets than his digital prowess could account for. Given everything he'd gone through, the fact that he was alive and sitting here today next to her was nothing short of a minor miracle. Brainjacks aside, he'd had more than his fair share of luck, and they both knew it. Rolling the dice again with his fate wasn't going to happen. Not on her watch.

"Let me think it over," Maddox said, attempting to ease the tension in the air.

"Thank you," Kipling said, then he stood up. "I'll drop by tomorrow morning, about this same time. We'll talk then." He bid them both a good morning and left.

When the door shut behind him, Maddox turned to Beatrice. "I think you could have been a bit more rude, yeah?"

Beatrice rolled her eyes. "God forbid someone look out for your best interests. Why would you even consider something like that? You just made the man's career. He owes you, not the other way around."

"He saved my life up on that roof," Maddox pointed out. "Or did you forget about that?"

"Right, he did save you. From a 'Nette who'd infiltrated his organization," she countered. "There was a good chance he was going to pull that trigger whether you'd been there or not. Tell me I'm wrong."

For once, Maddox didn't have a clever comeback.

Her arms still crossed, she said, "But forget all of that for a minute. I want you to tell me why you lied to the doctor just now."

Confused, he asked, "What are you talking about?"

"Don't deny it," Beatrice said, then pointed to her eyes. "These things are bullshit detectors now, remember? When she asked you if that connected feeling had hit you again, you said no. And that wasn't true, was it?"

Maddox's expression dropped. "No, it wasn't." Then he blew out a tired breath. "It didn't work. I can still feel that thing. And it's trying to get inside my head."

35
IF YOU DIE

It was just his mind playing tricks on him. That was what Maddox had thought initially, when he'd felt the first prickle of cybernetic connectivity the day after the procedure. The sensation was similar to what he'd felt before Wallbrink's attempt to disable his brainjacks, only much reduced. A whisper to a shout. And so he hadn't taken it seriously at first, blaming stress and mental exhaustion.

But the next day it had happened again, and stronger than before. Then once more later in the day. Still, he didn't tell the doctor, keeping it to himself and hoping against hope it was nothing but his imagination. Then that very morning, the third day after the procedure, he'd felt the strongest sensation yet, just before his morning checkup, and he'd finally admitted to himself it wasn't tension or anxiety or even paranoia. Whatever the medic had done to him, it seemed to have worked temporarily, but the effect was already beginning to wear off.

"You should have told the doctor," Beatrice reprimanded him, after he'd finally come clean with her.

"She'd only want to put me under the knife again," he said. "But you heard her just now. She's flying blind. She's never dealt with anything like this before, she said it herself. I'm not letting her poke around in my head again."

"You say that like you have an alternative."

"I do," Maddox said. Then he added, "Or maybe I do. I'm not sure yet."

"Not sure about what?" Beatrice asked, her expression as concerned as it was curious.

He gazed at her earnestly. "If I can help Kipling throw a net over that nameless AI, like he wants," Maddox said, "then we can turn the thing off. And if it's turned off, I don't have to worry about it getting in here." He tapped his temple with his finger.

Beatrice straightened up and regarded him skeptically. "Christ, salaryman. So now you think you can catch an AI? I know you're good at what you do, but isn't that just a bit beyond your reach?"

"Maybe," he admitted, pulling out a cigarette and lighting it, "on any other day." He blew smoke. "But I've got the FBI on my side now. So it just might be doable."

Leaning in closer to him, Beatrice grasped his forearm. "This is the part where I remind you there's another AI on the loose out there, and it's trying to take you out."

Maddox nodded. "I know there is. I'll be careful in there."

Furrowing her brow, Beatrice said, "In there? Wait, you're not thinking about actually plugging into VS, are you? That's suicide, Blackburn. You said as much yourself."

"I'll just have to be extra careful," he said, forcing far more conviction into his tone than he felt. A pointless effort, since Beatrice didn't seem to buy it for a second anyway.

A long silence passed between them. "And what if I ask you not to?" she asked. "What if I insist? Would you still do it?"

He stared down at his cigarette, a ribbon of smoke twisting upward. "No," he said after a moment. "I wouldn't."

"Listen to me," she said. "I want to see that machine's lights turned out as much as you do. Its people came after me too, you know. But I don't want to lose you, Blackburn."

He drew on his cigarette, staring down at the floor. "When I feel it, it's like I'm in a room in a building, and there's someone in the hallway, knocking on all the doors and calling my name, trying to find me, but they haven't yet. Eventually, though, they'll figure out which room I'm in, and no matter what I try to do to keep them out, they're going to break down the door and get inside." He blew smoke, lifted his eyes to meet hers. "I've seen it, you know. They way that machine changes people once it gets inside. I don't want to lose me either, Bea, but if I don't do something, that's exactly what's going to happen."

"Another doctor, then," Beatrice suggested. "A top brain specialist. We can find one."

"I don't think there's time for that." Before she could ask, he said, "Don't ask how I know. I can feel it. Those footsteps in the hallway are getting closer."

Another long quiet moment passed. "If there were any other path," he said, "trust me, I'd take it."

Beatrice let out a long sigh, finally seeming to give

in. "All right, then." She put his face in her hands, pulled him to her, and kissed him. "But if you die, salaryman, I'm going to fucking kill you, understand?"

Maddox grinned. "Got it."

The door opened and Tommy appeared. He lifted his chin as a greeting and stepped into the room. "So what did the doc say, bruh?" he asked Maddox. "Everything good?"

"Yes and no," Maddox said.

"What's that mean?" the kid asked, a worried expression knotting his face. "She find something wrong?"

"No, I'm fine," he assured the kid. "But I was thinking about taking matters into my own hands."

"What do you mean?" Tommy asked. "Like how?"

With a mischievous twinkle in his eye, Maddox said, "How'd you like to help me catch an AI?"

The kid's mouth dropped open slightly. He looked between Maddox and Beatrice with wide, disbelieving eyes. After a moment, he recovered himself, once again dropping into the detached, unflappable cool projected by every street kid since the beginning of time.

"Sure, bruh," he said with a shrug. "Sounds like fun."

36
WONDERLAND

Kipling had turned out to be a much easier sell than Beatrice. The next morning, when Maddox had explained to the FBI man what he had in mind, Kipling had jumped on board almost immediately.

"Brilliant," he'd praised the datajacker, suddenly animated by the possibility of finally capturing his white whale. "Yes, yes, that may very well work." Not wanting to waste a minute, Kipling had quickly arranged for security and transportation for the crosstown journey. By noon, everything had been arranged.

Now Maddox stood with Beatrice and Tommy, flanked by three security personnel, on the clinic's rooftop, waiting for their ride. Kipling, busy as ever, would catch up with them later at their destination.

"How are you feeling?" Beatrice asked him.

Sleep the previous night had come in restless bits and pieces, but thankfully he hadn't had a repeat of his disturbing dream—or visitation or whatever it had been—with the nameless AI. He seemed to have banished the entity—temporarily at least—from his subconscious by force of will. But he'd had two more of the waking *connectedness* episodes since yesterday, each more powerful and unsettling than the one before it. The footsteps in the hallway were definitely getting closer.

"Fine," he said, playing down his unease, though he knew Beatrice saw right through it. Fine for now, he qualified inwardly, but for how much longer? At what point would the machine take over his conscious mind? He felt it coming as inevitably as the next car's arrival at a subway station, but there was no way to know how long it would take. Something told him that car would arrive sooner than later.

Their ride, an armored hover, descended to the roof. Windows blackened and turbofans whining, it settled its bulky frame down onto the landing pad. Six more hovers floated nearby, forming a ring around the building's roof. Their security escort. Kipling had taken no chances with the trio's protection, taking every precaution imaginable, from removing all digital connectivity from the hovers (the drivers were operating on full manual) to arranging for a secure transit lane reserved only for his small fleet of authorized vehicles. They wouldn't be inconspicuous, but neither would they be an unusual sight in the City. Visiting heads of state often traveled by such means, as did a small number of uber-wealthy locals, those who could afford to pay the massive fees required to maintain their own private routes throughout the City's airways.

Minutes later, they were in the air, traveling northward under a sky of somber, overcast gray. They passed over the southernmost bend of the East River, its murky waters separating Brooklyn and Manhattan and held at bay by seawalls on both sides. Ground cars moved sluggishly along the Williamsburg bridge. Next to Maddox, Tommy had a sullen look on his face.

"What's wrong, kid?" Maddox asked.

"You sure you couldn't do this from the clinic?" the kid asked. "It *has* to be from that filthy hiverise?"

They'd gone over this earlier. "Sorry, kid. Like I said, it's the only setup in the City I know that might work."

"Don't mind him," Beatrice said. "He's thinking with his stomach, as usual." She nudged Tommy playfully with her elbow. "Poor baby. You going to miss your five-star breakfast in bed, are you?"

The kid gave her an annoyed look, then turned to the window. "Best green curry I ever had," he muttered.

When they reached the southern tip of Roosevelt Island, the hover banked gently to the left. Their destination appeared, looming in the near distance. Spanning several square blocks and home to countless thousands, the massive hiverise was the largest structure in view. A minute later, the armored hover touched down on the roof.

They'd arrive at Wonderland.

*   *   *

"When I said you were welcome here anytime, this wasn't exactly what I had in mind." Aziza, top dog at the hiverise known as Wonderland, sat behind a large desk in her spacious office, running her gaze across Maddox's armed security escort. True to how he remembered her, Aziza had remained calm and composed throughout the last confusing, undoubtedly stressful minutes. An unidentified armored hover had landed on her roof without permission, and half a dozen armed and armored federal agents had forced their way into her private offices and taken away her specs. Whenever he recalled his brief time here in Wonderland years ago, Maddox thought of the woman sitting across from him now as someone with more ice in her veins than anyone he'd ever known. Apparently, that hadn't changed. Her appearance hadn't either. Still fit and well muscled, still sporting the bleached white buzz cut that contrasted sharply with her dark skin.

"Sorry for showing up out of nowhere like this," he said. "But I couldn't call...for security reasons."

"So you're with the feds now?" she asked, glancing again at the trio of armed escorts behind him. Maddox had asked Beatrice and Tommy to wait for him in the anteroom beyond the door so Aziza wouldn't feel ganged up on. His security detail, under Kipling's strict orders not to leave the datajacker alone, had stayed with him.

"Not exactly," he said. "I'm helping them out with something."

"They twisting your arm?" she asked.

"No," he said, "it's nothing like that. I'm not in custody, not under investigation. We've got a...common interest. Maybe that's the best way to put it."

"And what exactly would that interest be?" Aziza asked.

"It's probably best you don't know all the details." Then he added, "For your own safety."

She lifted an eyebrow at him. "Really, jacker? You forget who you're talking to?"

He couldn't help but smile. "I'd tell you if I could,

I promise." Then, switching topics, he said, "Is this place still shielded and locked down like it was when I was here?" Aziza's predecessor, the infamous slumlord Rockefeller, had managed to suppress nearly all the hiverise's digital access to the outside world. Paranoid in the extreme and keen to control all communications within his fiefdom, he'd spent millions to have shielding plates and scrambling nodes installed throughout the massive structure, effectively cutting off all digital traffic within and beyond the hiverise's walls. Even old-school analog radio was impossible to use inside Wonderland. The only exception to this pervasive lockdown was a suite of small rooms, each with high-throughput connections enabled by physical cables. Only Rockefeller and his most trusted advisers were allowed access to these rooms, where they would conduct business with outside associates.

"We tried opening up for a few months," she said, then shook her head. "But it caused more problems than I ever imagined. Made me think old man Rock hadn't been that crazy after all. We got it locked down as tight as he ever did now. Maybe tighter."

"Still have those suites with cabled access to the outside?"

She nodded. "Still there, same as you remember."

Maddox felt a small surge of relief. It was exactly what he'd wanted to hear. Then he felt it. A tickle in the center of his mind. Like someone was whispering his name.

Blackburn, can you hear me? Blackburn?

He squeezed his eyes shut, shook his head, uncertain if he'd actually heard it or imagined it.

"You all right?" Aziza asked, in a way that made

him think it wasn't the first time she'd said it.

Opening his eyes, he rubbed his temples. "Killer headache," he said. "Didn't get much sleep last night." He removed a cigarette from the case in his jacket pocket and lit it.

"So, you think I could use those rooms for a few days?" he asked, blowing smoke.

Aziza ran her gaze once again across the security escort, then settled her eyes on Maddox. She cocked her head to one side and glared at him. "Do I have a choice in the matter?"

*   *   *

As Maddox had expected, Aziza was less than happy with the arrangement. She'd be fine in a few hours, Maddox knew, once she realized the feds had no interest in her or the hiverise empire she ruled over.

With Tommy's help, he spent the rest of the day working furiously in the cable-connected suites, testing and configuring gear provided by Kipling's department. It was all high-end stuff, worth more than Maddox ever could have afforded on his own. Sourced from local FBI offices throughout the City, most of equipment had arrived within a couple hours, shuttled to Wonderland in trucks disguised as food delivery vehicles. There were a few pieces of high-end hardware, though, only available at the D.C. office, and those were en route via one of the Bureau's jets.

Near midnight, Beatrice entered his and Tommy's work area in the second of the externally connected rooms. Boxes and packing foam were scattered everywhere, as were Tommy's carryout noodle containers.

"You two are filthy pigs," she said, wrinkling her

nose at the scene.

"Maid's on vacation, mama," Tommy joked as he twirled a trodeband around his finger. Then he spread his arms out wide. "Look at all this, B. You ever seen so much top-shelf gear in one place?"

"All I see is a mess," she said. Then to Maddox: "Come on, salaryman, you need to get some rest."

Lying back on an eggshell recliner, Maddox scrolled through a holo monitor floating above his head, ticking boxes and moving slider bars. He'd almost finished fine-tuning an array of high-capacity archives, a tedious task that had taken the better part of two hours. "Half an hour and I'm done," he said without looking away from his work.

"You're done now," she insisted. "Come on."

Maddox turned his head to find Beatrice looking down on him with her hands on her hips. From the determined look on her face, he knew arguing his case for more time would be a lost cause. He rubbed his eyes. He was too tired to argue anyway, inwardly admitting he badly needed a good night's sleep. He'd brought sleeping pills with him from Wallbrink's clinic. Tonight he wouldn't resist using them.

"All right, kid," he said. "Let's call it a day. The stuff we haven't knocked out yet, we can take care of in the morning." He got out of the recliner and stretched his aching back.

"Did you find out when Kipling's coming?" Beatrice asked.

"Noon tomorrow. One of the agents delivering hardware told me." To minimize detection risk, Kipling had limited his communication to word-of-mouth, using agents as messengers.

"Will you be ready by then?" Beatrice asked.

Maddox looked around at the mess of the room. "I know it doesn't look like it, but we're almost done."

"So it's going down tomorrow, then?" Beatrice asked. He heard the worry in her voice, saw it on her face.

"That's right," he said, trying to mask his own worry, but probably doing a poor job of it. "Tomorrow at noon we're going to catch an AI."

37

THE LITTLE BOT

At three in the morning, as it had done for every day for the last eighteen years, the little bot exited its cubbyhole and began its daily journey: a preset pattern over the polished granite floor. Though the large room's furnishings had changed and been moved dozens of times over the years, requiring the little bot to adapt to new obstacles, the baseline cleaning pattern had not been altered since the bot had been brought into service nearly two decades earlier. Tonight it would finish the job in less time than normal, since its sweepers had been recently replaced. Fifteen seconds less, perhaps twenty or thirty—it depended on if there were new obstacles to negotiate or not. But time didn't matter to the little bot. All it cared about was doing a complete job.

The little bot was a sturdy model, built to last. Its chassis had lots of dents and scrapes from unexpected run-ins with rats and feral cats, but still it ran and ran and never needed any repairs or replacement parts—aside from its sweepers and cleaning brushes, which were designed to be replaced routinely. It had done its job so thoroughly, so dependably over the years that its owners had long ago stopped bothering to speak to it. The little bot didn't mind, though. That wasn't important. Cleaning the floor was important.

But if its owner, whoever that was, had chosen to talk with the little bot, he or she would have found its microphone still in pristine working order. Just like the rest of the little bot, the mic was also built to last. And so was its transceiver, the part that could receive and transmit wireless commands. But like the microphone, the transceiver hadn't been used in ages either. It seemed the little bot was so good at its job, all of its advanced capabilities were no longer needed. The little bot didn't mind, though. It didn't care about such things. It only cared about cleaning the floor.

If it *had* cared, though, it might have been relieved when it was finally spoken to again, after so many years of silence. Two days earlier, a bumblebee drone had found a way into the room where the little bot's cubbyhole was and had begun to speak to it. The drone asked the bot to listen carefully, day and night, for specific things. The name Maddox was one of these things, though the little bot didn't think of it as a name, only as a specific audio profile, a digitized translation of the vibrations picked up by its tiny condenser microphone. And because it also possessed a nearly forgotten voice-recognition software upgrade, the little bot had also been asked to listen for specific voice patterns. The drone gave it several templates to listen for. One for Maddox, one for Beatrice, one for Kipling, and another for Tommy, though again, it didn't think of them in terms of voices or names, only as digitized audio patterns. Since the drone's instructions didn't interfere with its cleaning duties, the little bot was only too happy to oblige.

The little bot had no capacity for amazement, but if it had, it would have been surprised to find matches for almost every one of those patterns the very next day! The name Maddox was uttered several dozen times, and the voices of Maddox, Tommy, and Beatrice had all been positively recognized, with a certainty factor of ninety-nine point eight percent. Yes, its microphone and transceiver were truly built to last. That very same day, just as the bot was finishing its cleaning pattern (thirty-five seconds early, thank you very much), another bumblebee drone arrived to see if the little bot had heard anything. If the bot had had the capacity to speculate on it, it might have guessed that thousands of other tiny drones had been dispatched throughout the City on similar errands, asking countless domestic bots far and wide to listen for the same things the little bot had been listening for.

But only one, the little bot that had been built to last, that for years had faithfully cleaned the granite floor of the penthouse in the Wonderland hiverise, returned what the master of all those drones, the Latour-Fisher AI, had been ceaselessly searching for.

Blackburn Maddox had been found.

** END OF BOOK FOUR **

The action continues in THE DATA RIOT, the final chapter in the Cyberpunk City saga. Turn the page for a preview of the opening chapters.

CYBERPUNK CITY BOOK FIVE: THE DATA RIOT

Forced by a fringe AI cult to undergo an irreversible procedure, Maddox's mind will never be the same. But in a dark twist of fate, his cybernetically-enhanced brain—the irreversible upgrade he never asked for and never wanted—may hold the key to ending the AI wars for good, and altering humanity's fate forever.

PROLOGUE

Five Years Ago

From the moment Maddox woke up, he knew something bad was going to happen that day. Something just felt off. He tried to ignore it, that sense of foreboding, of looming disaster as he drank his morning coffee and munched on toasted bread. He told himself it had to be the breakup. It still had him down, making him see everything in a negative light.

Two weeks had passed since he'd left Lora and rented his own place. The transition had been harder than he'd imagined, and the darkness of his moods— even by his own fatalistic standards—had reached lows he hadn't thought possible. Before he'd packed up and left her, he'd thought the breakup would bring peace of mind, or at the very least some sense of a burden removed. But it hadn't been like that at all. After living with someone two years, splitting up was going to be rough, no matter how bad you thought things were. Rooney had told him that, and the old man hadn't been wrong.

Finishing his coffee, Maddox rolled a cigarette and lit it. He had to get his head together. Time, Roon had assured him. Nothing but time would fix it.

His specs began to blink on the breakfast table. The old man's custom chime. Maddox blew smoke, reached for his lenses. What would Roon want at this hour?

"We got a gig," Rooney said a moment later. "I need you to get over here asap."

Maddox swallowed the last of his coffee. "A gig?" He'd spent three hours testing new gear at Rooney's place the day before, and the old man had never mentioned any jobs in the pipeline. "Why didn't you tell me about this yesterday?"

"Because it wasn't on the radar yesterday," Rooney said. The old man's call icon was a small Everton Football Club logo, and it pulsed as he spoke. "It's a rush job, boyo."

Blowing smoke, Maddox frowned. He didn't like rush jobs. They were messy, slapdash affairs. Lead time was essential in their business. You needed time to make dry runs in a test environment, to come up with contingency plans, to tweak apps and modify your gear. The more time you had to plan, the less you ended up leaving to chance, and the less likely you'd wind up in jail or brainspiked by some vicious watchdog AI.

Maddox knew Rooney wouldn't answer any questions over the connection. Even though theirs was a tightly encrypted call between burner specs with stacks of fake IDs, you could never be too careful. And being careful had kept them out of jail—and neurologically undamaged—over the decade they'd worked together, while so many of their peers had ended up in prison or brain-dead or dead dead. Maddox would have to get his answers face-to-face, within the shielded privacy of Rooney's condo in Queens.

"All right," Maddox said, crushing out his cigarette. "Be there in an hour."

* * *

From his newly rented condo in Midtown Manhattan, it would have taken Maddox forever to get to Queens on the subway—forever and a day in a ground car—so he called a hover cab, seeing as Rooney seemed to be in a hurry. As he climbed into the driverless vehicle on his building's fiftieth-floor pickup vestibule, he reminded himself to insist Rooney reimburse him for the added expense.

Dense traffic clogged the transit lanes, though not quite as bad as it would have been an hour earlier, during the height of morning rush hour. The cab crawled its way along, a tiny fish lost among scores of others, swimming in automated formation along the invisible avenues of the sky. Higher and higher they went, stacks of traffic reaching a hundred stories and more, each horizontal layer thinner and less transited than the one below it.

To give himself time for one last smoke—Rooney never let him light up inside—Maddox had the hover drop him off a couple of blocks from his mentor's address in Jackson Heights. Now he walked along an ancient walkway that was more gone than there, a trampled path of weeds and overgrowth where there had once been a paved sidewalk. It was so different here, he reflected, taking in his surroundings. Hard to believe where he stood was only a handful of miles from Times Square. In this part of Queens, there were no hiverises, no hover-clogged arteries filling the sky above your head, not even much ground traffic. And if it weren't for the constant noise of aircraft coming and going at nearby LaGuardia Airport, the place would have been something of a quiet little oasis. And even with the perpetual whine of jet engines, Jackson Heights still managed to feel like a small haven of sorts, a respite from the City's tireless motion.

Rooney had moved to the location two years earlier, having had enough of Manhattan's constant bustle and flow. At forty-three, Rooney wasn't old for most occupations, but he was ancient in the datajacking business, whose practitioners rarely made it past their thirtieth birthday before their luck ran out. A small minority managed to leave the biz with their health and freedom intact, cashing out after some big-money windfall of a gig, but these cases were very much the exception to the rule. Most often, a datajacker's career ended in prison or the morgue. Still, the few success stories were enough to keep hope alive across the profession, much in the same way lottery players believed—against all statistical odds to the contrary—that someday they'd eventually hold a winning ticket.

Maddox held no such illusions. He knew his profession was a short-lived one. What worried him—both for his sake and the old man's—was that Rooney didn't seem to share this belief. And lately this worried Maddox more and more.

Because the old man was slipping. Over the last year Rooney had made a dozen or more little screw-ups and missteps—and the occasional near-devastating blunder—while they'd been on the job. The kind of stuff that would have been unimaginable earlier in his career. Rookie mistakes like forgetting to tweak his cloaking app, making him so easy to detect that some low-cost off-the-shelf antivirus software would spot him. Or he'd cut corners on prep work, neglecting to simulate some scenario or other in the test environment. And then later, when those untested situations cropped up on a job, he and Maddox had to scramble to keep things from taking a disastrous turn.

At first, Maddox had ignored it, telling himself no one was perfect. Everyone messed up once in a while. But then the incidents became too frequent to dismiss, and too perilous for Maddox to remain quiet about it. Months ago, after their most recent job, Maddox had suggested maybe it was time for Rooney to retire, and his mentor had lashed out at him. What the hell did he know? the old man had shot back. He'd been jacking data since Maddox was in diapers. Afterward, Maddox realized he'd touched a nerve. Datajackers egos are fragile things, and it couldn't have been easy for the teacher to have his failures called out by the student. Since then, Maddox hadn't brought up the subject.

Maddox flicked his cigarette away and pressed the button for Rooney's unit; the buzzer unlocked the door. He entered the building and began the five-flight climb to Rooney's place. Ever the tightfisted bargain hunter, the old man had rented the elevator-less building's cheapest unit, located on the top floor.

As Maddox ascended the stairs, the sinking feeling he'd woken up with was still with him. The meat was trying to tell him something, and sometimes the meat knew more than the mind. It was funny like that. As he reached Rooney's unit and knocked on the door, he steeled himself for the inevitable fight to come. But he had to do it. For the old man's own good, he'd convince Roon to hang up his datajacking gear for good.

* * *

"Easy money, boyo," Rooney said, wearing a fuzzy gray robe and slippers and standing in his small kitchen. He poured a cup of coffee for his guest. "Easiest we've come across in a while." Maddox sat on a stool at the breakfast bar. The place was a wreck, as usual. Datajacking equipment was lying around everywhere. Sloppy piles of trodebands, VS decks in various stages of deconstruction—or construction, Maddox couldn't tell—their chassis opened, revealing complicated innards crammed full of tiny components. Tools and food wrappers and stacks of dishes in the sink. Chez Rooney as it always had been and always would be: an aging bachelor's den of slovenly disorganization. Maddox, whose innate tidiness put him closer to the neat-freak end of the spectrum, had once told his mentor that if he set off a grenade in the middle of his flat, no one would be able to tell the difference.

"Fence job," Rooney said. "Simple as they come."

"Who's the client?" Maddox asked.

Rooney slid the coffee to Maddox, who accepted it with a nod. "We didn't get that far," Rooney replied.

"What do you mean?"

"I mean it's a blind gig," Rooney said.

Maddox frowned and blew steam off his coffee before sipping it. It was yet another slip, yet another ill-advised shortcut.

While it wasn't unheard of to work a gig where you didn't know the client's identity, on those occasions Rooney and Maddox had always made every effort to find out exactly who they were dealing with. Undercover stings were a regular occurrence in their business, so you couldn't be too careful. Rooney apparently hadn't lifted a finger to find out who the hiring party was.

"I know, I know," Rooney said, seeing the other's reaction. "But it's just a simple fence job. We take the dataset, shop it around, and take a thirty percent cut when we sell it."

"*Thirty* percent?" The normal rate was half that.

Rooney smiled devilishly. "That's right. They want a rush job," he said, rubbing his forefinger and thumb together, "they gotta pay a premium."

"How rushed are we talking about here?" Maddox asked.

"We have to take possession asap," Rooney answered, explaining how the client had left the IP in a less-than-secure public archive in virtual space. It was like leaving a cache of stolen diamonds wrapped in a towel on the sidewalk. Sooner or later someone was bound to notice it, pick it up, and walk away with it.

"And what were you planning to do about standbys?" Maddox asked, not liking what he'd heard so far. Their regular standbys, a couple named Buddy and Pris, were on holiday in Thailand.

Rooney shrugged. "We'll be in and out in two

minutes. It's not like we're breaking into some locked-down DS, boyo."

Maddox grunted in disapproval. Plugging in without standbys—even for just a couple minutes—was like walking a tightrope ten stories up without a net. As the role's name implied, standbys literally stood next to a datajacker when he was connected to virtual space, monitoring the jacker's biofeedback—especially brain activity—for any signs of trouble. If something went wrong, a standby would physically remove the jacker's trodeband, manually unplugging them from VS. Buddy and Pris had been Maddox and Rooney's reliable standbys for years.

"Less than ideal," Rooney said. "I know."

Understatement of the decade, Maddox complained inwardly. "What kind of data are we talking about?"

"Pharma R&D," Rooney said. "Fortune 50 outfit."

At least the old man had found out that much, Maddox noted. "So it ought to fetch a good price."

"My thoughts exactly."

Maddox drank his coffee. "I don't like it, Roon."

"Not the best circumstances, I admit, but the known risk is negligible."

"Negligible?" Maddox scoffed. "How do you figure that?"

"Ira Domnitz brought it to us," Rooney said. "How much work has he steered our way over the years? And not once has he ever screwed us over."

Maddox couldn't disagree there. Domnitz was as reliable as they came. An attorney by trade, he specialized in handling the messy, complex legal separations of wealthy corporati from their employers. Sometimes his clients parted ways with their firms holding a valuable cache of not-so-legally-obtained intellectual property. For a percentage of the proceeds, he was happy to help them unload the IP via his friends who worked in the shadowy world of the black market. Rooney had known the attorney for decades, and their business relationship was watertight.

"And Ira didn't tell you the client name?" Maddox prodded.

"He usually does, I know." Rooney conceded, then he shrugged. "But he was giving me the 'attorney-client privilege' routine. I didn't press him for it."

Again, Maddox frowned. "Why not?"

"Because like I said," Rooney snapped, a bit defensively, "he's never steered us wrong before, has he?"

"Things only have to go wrong once," Maddox pointed out, using the phrase Rooney had often employed himself, though not very much lately.

Rooney set his cup down on the counter with a frustrated thud. "You want to tell me why you're so wound up about this job, boyo?"

Maddox took a breath, longing for a smoke. "It's not just this job, Roon. It's all of them."

"All of them?"

"All of them lately, I mean," Maddox qualified. "Cutting corners on prep work, taking unnecessary risks when we're in VS. The kind of stuff you never used to do before. The kind of stuff that gets people busted, or worse." He paused, then added, "And you've been forgetting things."

Rooney's mouth tightened into a straight line. "You coming back to this again?" he snapped. "You think I'm slipping?" He tapped his temple. "Think something's wrong up here?"

"I'm just worried, Roon."

"Think it's time for me to get out, do you?"

"I think it's long past time, if you want to know the truth," Maddox said bluntly. Then he braced himself for the backlash that was sure to come. Except that it didn't. The anger drained from Rooney's expression. Then his gaze dropped to the countertop, and for a long time neither of them spoke.

"You think I don't know that?" Rooney finally said with a sigh. "But I need this gig, Blackburn. We haven't worked in over three months, and things are tight for me right now. Really tight."

Maddox furrowed his brow. "You don't have anything put away?"

"I did," Rooney said, then gestured around. "And then I bought this place."

"If it's just about the cash, I can float you for a while," Maddox suggested, but even as he said it, he knew what Rooney's prideful reaction would be.

"I don't need your charity, boyo. I need to work."

Maddox finished his coffee, then set his cup down. "A blind gig, taken on a moment's notice, with no standbys," he said. "It's the kind of job you would have rejected out of hand once upon a time."

"I know, I know," Rooney admitted sheepishly. "And I know I'm not as sharp as I used to be. I'm no idiot, Blackburn. I see it, same as you do. But this is the only life I've ever known, and stepping away from it…" His voice trailed off.

"Isn't easy," Maddox said.

"No, it's not."

Rooney wasn't the sentimental sort. Maddox had liked that about him from the beginning. The old man was brutally honest, practical, and he never allowed emotion to cloud his decisions. So it came as no surprise when the moment of self-pity passed quickly, and Rooney straightened his back and gazed steadily at his longtime apprentice with clear eyes.

"So all right, then," Rooney said decisively. "Last job. After this one, I'll figure something else out."

Maddox looked at him skeptically. "Are you serious?"

"Payout on this gig's going to keep me in the black for half a year," Rooney said. "I can use the time to figure out another line of work." He rinsed out his coffee cup in the sink, placed it on a towel. "I won't lie to you, Blackburn. I've been thinking about getting out. More than you know." He smiled faintly. "Maybe I needed a bit of a push. So I guess I should thank you for that, boyo."

Resisting the urge to sigh in relief, Maddox nodded and returned the smile. Only minutes earlier, he'd been wound up in knots, worried the conversation would go in a very different direction. He was still wary of this rushed job for some anonymous client, to be sure, but if it got Roon out of the game for good, it was a risk worth taking.

And was it really *that* risky, after all? They'd done this kind of thing dozens of times, and never once had anything gone wrong. But then his own words—preached to him so many times by Rooney it was like a mantra—repeated themselves in his head.

Things only have to go wrong once.

* * *

As it turned out, it took less than five seconds for

things to go wrong, for all hell to break loose. Moments after they'd plugged into virtual space, near the location where the client had stored the IP for them to recover, something hit them. Something big. A cybernetic monster unlike anything Maddox had ever seen or felt. It was like a building fell on top of him. Back in the room, his body went as rigid as petrified wood. He couldn't move a finger. His mind was held tightly in the thing's grip. He couldn't think, couldn't subvocalize any commands, couldn't even remember his own name. There was only animal panic, bursting forth from the depths of his lower brain. Then after what felt like a long stretch of agonizing terror—but had perhaps been no more than a few moments—Maddox opened his eyes.

He gasped for breath, reaching to touch his face, his body, to make sure he was really there, really out of VS. Christ, he'd almost bought it. What the hell had jumped him? An AI? What would an AI be doing hanging around a public archive? Or had there been a wicked glitch with their gear? The mother of all glitches.

He lay there, taking large breaths, feeling his heart beat wildly but then finally begin to slow.

"Roon?" he said. "You all right?"

From somewhere nearby, Maddox heard the old man moan. The muscles in his neck were still too stiff and tingling to turn and look. Aftereffects of whatever had happened to him in VS.

"My head's killing me, boyo," Rooney groaned.

Maddox felt his neck muscles begin to loosen up. So the bad vibes he'd had about this gig hadn't been off base after all. At least they'd made it out. And miraculously so, without the aid of standbys.

"Where the hell are we?" Rooney asked.

"What do you mean—" Maddox began to ask but then stopped, suddenly confused by what he was staring at. Above him was cracked, crumbling concrete where the white-paneled ceiling of Rooney's condo should have been. And underneath his body, instead of the soft contours of the egg recliner, he felt like he was lying on something flat and hard. With an effort, Maddox sat up and looked around, shocked to find himself in a jail cell.

Where the hell am I? he thought. The space was tiny, barely large enough for the narrow bed he was sitting on. The cement floor and walls were identical to the ceiling, old and in an advanced state of crumbling decay. The air was damp and smelled vaguely of salt and brine. Beyond the rusted iron bars of his cell, across a separating walkway, Rooney sat on an identical bed, in an identical cell.

Maddox automatically reached for his trodeband, finding nothing around his head. He looked down at his hands, rubbed his fingers together. He ran his tongue over his teeth. If this was a simulation, it was the most realistic one he'd ever seen. Was he hallucinating? Had something happened to him in VS, triggering a bizarre waking dream?

He looked over at Rooney again. "Roon, what's going on?"

Anxiety twisted his mentor's expression. "We're still in VS, boyo," Rooney said. "And I think we just got caught."

1
LEFTOVER NOODLES

Waking with a gasp, Maddox sat up quickly in bed and looked around in a panic. He saw no bars, no decaying cement floors and walls. Outside the window, it was still dark, and the faint whine of early-morning hover traffic came through the walls. Beside him, Beatrice slept, snoring lightly.

Wonderland, he remembered. That was where he was. The hiverise called Wonderland. Just to be sure, he pinched himself, wincing from the pain but at the same time welcoming it. Real pain, not simulated pain. He blew out a breath and felt his racing heart begin to slow. Far too awake now to go back to sleep, he quietly rose and made his way to the shower.

Weeks had passed since he'd last had the recurring dream, a replay of his and Rooney's capture and confinement by the Latour-Fisher AI. The entity had placed them in a virtual prison, where it had slowed down perceived time to such a degree that a few days had seemed like endless months of captivity. Maddox had survived the ordeal, Rooney hadn't. Now, five years removed from Rooney's death, Maddox wondered if the dream would ever stop haunting him, if it would ever stop dosing him with fresh portions of guilt and self-loathing he'd carry with him for days afterward. He would have done almost anything to cure himself of the dream, to heal the damaged part of his mind that wouldn't allow him to forget how badly he'd screwed up that day. How he'd ignored every warning bell going off in his head and let his friend take on that fatal job.

Sorry, boyo. I'd stop those dreams if I could.

Maddox grinned woefully as he showered. With the sour came the sweet. Rooney's death had broken something inside him, and the damage manifested itself not only with the curse of his recurring dream, but also with the blessing of his late mentor's voice. Though he knew it was his own subconscious projection over which he had no control, it still comforted him to hear Rooney in his head from time to time. In a warped kind of way, the auditory hallucinations were reassuring. It was almost like the old man was still around.

Taking care not to wake Beatrice, Maddox toweled off, dressed in the hazy predawn light, then padded out of the small suite. Closing the door behind him, he donned a pair of burner specs and amped up the light sensitivity so he could see his way through the dark winding corridors. By now he'd memorized the route to the interconnected rooms that had become his workplace, but he still needed the extra light. You never knew what might be left lying around, waiting to be stepped on. Drug needles, cockroaches, or—in the nicer parts of the hiverise—cleaner bots making their nightly rounds.

Minutes later, he was checking the gear he'd set up

the day before. With the dream still fresh in his mind, he obsessively ran diagnostics on all the physical connections, validated and revalidated the app settings he'd tweaked hours earlier, and tested scenario after scenario in an offline sandbox environment. Before he knew it, two hours had passed.

"You have breakfast already?"

He started at Beatrice's disembodied voice. Gesturing, he exited the offline construct and his awareness returned to the room. Beatrice stood in the doorway, a pair of takeaway food boxes in her hands.

"No," Maddox said. "Not yet."

"Come on, take a break," she said, apparently aware he'd been at it for some time. "You know what they say: can't catch an AI on an empty stomach."

Maddox hadn't eaten since last night, and he was suddenly aware of the gnawing emptiness in his belly. They sat at the room's only table. Beatrice slid one of the boxes toward him and handed him a pair of chopsticks.

"Just leftovers I grabbed from the fridge," she said. "I warmed them up."

Maddox swirled the steaming noodles around with his chopsticks. "The Tommy Park special, huh?"

Beatrice slurped a mouthful from her box. "Seriously, have you ever seen the kid eat anything else?"

"I brought him some fresh vegetables once," Maddox said.

"No way he ate them."

Maddox shook his head and chuckled. "Biggest fight we ever had. You would have thought I'd asked him to drink toilet water, the way he flipped out."

For a while, they ate without speaking. Under any other circumstance, it would have been a pleasant breakfast: just him and Beatrice, enjoying a peaceful morning together. But the difficult and dangerous task ahead of him, weighing heavily on his mind, spoiled the moment.

Capturing an AI. Was it even possible? As far as he knew, it had never even been attempted. He had the best gear and apps money could buy at his disposal, but still, he was far from certain he could pull it off. He believed his trap *could* work, but would it? He wondered what Rooney might have said about it.

You don't know want to know, boyo.

"Shut up," Maddox said.

"Excuse me?" Beatrice said, straightening up.

"Sorry. Didn't mean to say that out loud."

"The old man giving you a hard time?" she asked.

"A bit." Maddox had told her how his old mentor's voice haunted him. Thankfully, she hadn't thought him insane, telling him it was most likely post-traumatic something-or-other. After what he'd been through, she'd said, it would have been surprising if he hadn't had any psychological damage. A mercenary by trade, Beatrice had seen—and dealt with herself once or twice—the mental aftereffects of traumatic events.

She gazed at him intently. "Anything else going on up there?"

Maddox knew what she was referring to. "Not right now," he said.

Unconsciously, he reached up and touched the small bandage behind his ear that covered the brainjacks. Forced upon him by an underground AI cult for reasons he still didn't understand, the unwanted—and globally banned—neural implants of this type typically served dual purposes. First, they enhanced mental capabilities, effectively supercharging the human mind. Want to understand dozens of languages you'd never learned or didn't know the first word of? There was a ware for that, and all you had to do was slide it into one of your brainjack slots. Learn advanced mathematics in a day. Fill your head with a library of books in minutes. There were wares for those too, all designed by the cult's nameless AI leader for the benefit of its faithful followers.

The implants' second, more insidious aim was to allow the cult's AI full, unfettered access to your mind. At any given moment, the nameless AI could sense every firing neuron in your head, perceive your every thought and desire and emotion, conscious or otherwise. This access was the crux of the movement's creed: the belief that with the AI's benevolent guidance, empowered by its all-seeing view of their consciousness, its followers could maximize their potential, making optimal life decisions and following their customized path of highest personal enlightenment. Maddox had heard the movement's bullshit dogma countless times, long before he'd had brainjacks drilled into his skull. His ex, Lora, was among the nameless AI's followers, a so-called 'Nette. The pejorative—short for "marionette"—implied the movement's adherents were nothing more than puppets, gullible dupes controlled by a superintelligent machine.

What worried Maddox the most about unwanted implants was that they enabled two-way communication, a kind of digital telepathy, between the nameless AI and "those to whom it was connected." If the 'Nettes' movement could be thought of as a religion, then this was how they prayed. And unlike the deities of other religions, the cybernetic god of the 'Nettes actually spoke back to its believers. Shortly after having his brainjacks implanted, Maddox had undergone a procedure to obstruct the nameless AI's access to his mind. At first, it had seemed to work, but the blocking effect had turned out to be temporary. Lately he'd begun to sense the machine's presence, trying to undo what the medical staff had done, trying to gain access to his mind. With each passing hour, he felt with absolute certainty the machine was getting closer, that his time as a free-thinking human being was running out. Every so often, an unsettling sense of connectedness would hit him, reminding him of the urgency of the task before him. If he didn't capture the nameless AI and destroy it, then soon his mind would no longer be his own.

"Smells good in here." Tommy Park, Maddox's datajacking apprentice, entered the room and sat at the table. "So what are we having this morning?" He looked back and forth longingly between the two boxes of noodles, reminding Maddox of the way a stray dog stares at a food stand's diners in hopes of a free meal.

Beatrice removed some cash from her pocket and slid it across the table. "There's a food court two levels down."

The kid smiled and pocketed the bills. "Thanks, mama." The grin faded as Tommy turned to Maddox. "So this is really going down today, bruh?"

"That's the plan," Maddox said.

Tommy fidgeted in his chair. "We went kinda fast on the prep, yeah? Think we might need more time for configs and testing and such?"

Maddox looked up from his noodles. "You getting cold feet on me, kid?"

"It's not that, boss," Tommy said, coolly ignoring the jab at his ego. A year earlier, Maddox reflected, the kid would have puffed out his chest, lifted his chin, and boasted that he wasn't afraid of anything. Tommy Park was growing up, it seemed.

"This ain't some corporate DS or encrypted archive we're going up against," Tommy continued. "I mean, one day of prep to take on an AI? We prep for two days, minimum, on small jobs with cheapo security and off-brand countermeasures."

"We're ready," Maddox said, his tone more defensive than he'd intended. The kid and Beatrice exchanged a worried look. "We're ready," Maddox insisted, addressing them both. "Trust me."

"We trust you," Beatrice said, then added gently, "but we think you might be rushing things. With what they did to you, I can understand how badly you'd want to—"

"You don't understand," Maddox interrupted. He removed his tobacco bag from his jacket pocket and began to roll a cigarette. "You have no idea what it's like."

As he finished rolling his smoke and lit it, Beatrice remained silent. Then she said, "You're right. I don't know. But if Tommy thinks you're moving too fast, maybe you should listen."

Annoyed, Maddox blew smoke. Annoyed not because she and Tommy were wrong, but because they were right. He *had* hurried things along. He'd skipped over a hundred tiny details he'd typically check twice or even three times. He'd disregarded several checklists that had been part of his normal prep routine for years. All of it to save a handful of hours. In his desperation to block the AI from gaining control of his mind before it was too late, he'd thrown together his cybernetic trap quickly, perhaps too quickly. Maybe even sloppily, if he was being honest with himself.

Still, if he'd acted hastily, it was because time was against him. Obsessive testing and scenario planning were luxuries he couldn't afford right now. At any moment he could lose control of his own thoughts. Lose himself. No, he thought, if anything he hadn't been moving fast enough.

As if to remind him, the unsettling sense of connectedness once again overcame him. For a moment he felt as if he was in some other place, alone in some other room, and just beyond the door, he could hear people milling about and whispering his name. He sensed that at any moment, the door would fly open and the mob would surge inside like when the doors open on a crowded subway car. And then he'd be overwhelmed. Lost.

"Bruh," Tommy said, nudging his mentor's shoulder. "You all right?"

Maddox snapped out of it, taking a long draw on his cigarette. It had been the strongest such episode yet. "I'm fine," he said unconvincingly. Then he shifted his gaze between Beatrice and Tommy. "I know I'm moving fast on this," he admitted. "Maybe faster than I should. But it's only because I know I don't have much time before…" He couldn't bring himself to finish the sentence.

Beatrice grasped his forearm. "Just be careful, yeah?"

"I will," he said, the faint voices whispering his name still echoing in his mind. "I promise."

"Yeah, we'll definitely be careful," Tommy added.

Maddox gave the kid a sharp look. "Sorry, kid. This one's a solo run."

Tommy looked gut-punched. "What?"

"I need you as my standby. If things go sideways in there, you'll need to pull me out quick."

The kid pointed a thumb at Beatrice. "She can stand by for both of us. You're gonna need all the help you can get in there, boss."

Maddox shook his head resolutely. "You know what to look for. You can spot something going wrong long before she can. I need you on the outside, Tommy. That's where you can help the most."

The kid didn't look happy about it, but he didn't argue, knowing Maddox had a point. Tommy had worked alongside his mentor the entire previous day, designing and constructing the AI trap, so he knew how it would work—or how it was supposed to work—down to the last detail. Which meant the kid also knew his presence inside the partitioned slice of virtual space was unnecessary and redundant.

There was a loud knock, and the trio turned in unison to see the door swing open. Two men wearing in suits and large dark specs entered the room. They quickly scanned the premises, then one of them turned and nodded. "All clear," he announced.

FBI Director Stellan Kipling appeared, briskly stepping through the doorway and dismissing his security detail to the corridor. Kipling, a short pudgy man who seemed less like a law enforcement professional than a disheveled intellectual, ran the Bureau's Data Crimes division, and he'd become Maddox's unlikely ally in the datajacker's struggle to free himself from the cross fire of two warring AIs. For years, Kipling had tracked the nameless AI whose existence had been nothing more than an urban legend, a kind of cybernetic Bigfoot or Lock Ness monster only conspiracy theorists believe in. His colleagues had teased him incessantly over his obsession, dubbing him a ghost hunter. Only until these last few days, when he'd managed to arrest several of the AI's brainjacked followers in a raid, had his efforts been vindicated. And now, with Maddox's help, he hoped to capture the 'Nettes' benefactor, the nameless rogue AI he'd been hunting for years like his own personal white whale, and bring it under his control.

The look on the man's face said it all, Maddox noted inwardly as Kipling bid them all good morning. He was brimming with energy, his eyes clear and sharp and full of purpose. Maddox wished he could have shared the man's confidence, his enthusiasm.

Kipling rubbed his hands together and smiled widely. "It feels like a good day to catch an AI, wouldn't you say?"

END OF PREVIEW

Hope you enjoyed this preview of THE DATA RIOT, the fifth and final book in the CYBERPUNK CITY series.

ACKNOWLEDGEMENTS

My sincerest thanks to Audie Wallbrink and Ki Harrison. Your early input to the story was invaluable!

Thanks also to my editors, Holly Walrath and Eliza Dee.

ABOUT THE AUTHOR

D.L. Young is a Texas-based author. He's a Pushcart Prize nominee and winner of the Independent Press Award. His stories have appeared in many publications and anthologies.

For free books, new release updates, and exclusive previews, visit his website at www.dlyoungfiction.com.

Printed in Great Britain
by Amazon

62507186R00154